Vickie

Vickie

MIKE SIMS

Volume one of the Vickie series

Vickie

Copyright © 2016 by Mike Sims. All rights reserved.

No part of this publication may be reproduced, stored in a retrieval system or transmitted in any way by any means, electronic, mechanical, photocopy, recording or otherwise without the prior permission of the author except as provided by USA copyright law.

This novel is a work of fiction. Names, descriptions, entities, and incidents included in the story are products of the author's imagination. Any resemblance to actual persons, events, and entities is entirely coincidental. The opinions expressed by the author are not necessarily those of Mazzaroth.

Published by Mazzaroth
Katy, TX
www.Mazzaroth.net

Published in the United States of America

ISBN: 978-0-9982983-7-5
Fiction / Drama

To Jean Pickering and Marlene Thomas
at Capstone Classical Academy.

Acknowledgments

Thank you, Nicole Andani, for your wisdom and support in making this book and its series a reality.

Contents

In the Beginning...

I T IS A hot summer day on a long endless stretch of road. The Newsome family are on their way to moving near some of their family to start again. Tom and Mary as well as eight-year-old Vickie are enduring the long journey to a hopeful destination of Tom's brother Dan. Times had driven them from their home as they made their escape with what money they have and their few possessions dragging behind them in a trailer. Like a modern-covered wagon, they head west to find a new life and new start. Tom Newsome knows he should be heading elsewhere but has managed to lose his way. His wife tells him to pull out the interstate and see if they can find a map or directions. This violates his sense of manhood but eventually realizes it is a lost cause. He drives down a lonely road away from the interstate and sees a crossroad and a small rundown gas station.

As he pulls into a gas station, the attendant begins to walk up to the car.

"Howdy," says the attendant.

"Hi yourself," Tom replies. "Say do you know how to get to Hemdale? We are not far, I know, but not sure which way to go."

Attendant responds, "You want to take the road to the right, follow it to Sands and then left on 88. That will take you straight to Hemdale."

Tom says, "Thank you, sir."

The attendant looks at the young girl in the back and asks, "Why, who might you be?"

The girl looks away shy and blushing while her mom Mary responds, "Vickie, answer the nice man."

The attendant responds, "Vickie, what a nice name for a pretty girl. You know I have a feeling you're going to grow up to be a very important person."

Vickie looks at the man as he intently stares back and quietly says, "Yes, indeed, you will make a huge difference in many." A silence creeps in as only the sound of desert wind blows.

Mary looked at the attendant then Vickie and then to Tom. "Well, honey, don't you think we should be going?" She turns to the attendant, "Thank you, sir, for your guidance."

The attendant slowly looks back at the parents and says, "No problem, ma'am, you people have a safe trip." The attendant backs away as the Newsomes begin to move their car forward.

Vickie stares at the man as he nods his head yes at her. Vickie looks confused but curious as the man never stops staring the whole time they drive away. She stares back as far as she can.

Vickie asked, "Mom, who is that man?"

Mary answered, "Just a man who runs a gas station."

"He looks like I have seen him before."

"You just remember seeing someone like him, we have never been around here before."

"What was he telling me?"

"I think he was trying to be nice to you."

Tom interrupts, "You two need to shut up. I am trying to concentrate on the road and don't need a lot of chitchat."

A silence befalls them for a while and Mary asks, "Honey, would you like the radio on?"

Tom says, "If it would shut that trap of yours."

Mary says, "Do you have to talk like that to me?"

"Look, I'm trying to keep us alive and fed which is a bit hard when you bitches won't leave me alone."

"Tom, do you have to use such language in front our child?"

"You bring it out me. I can't wait to get to my brother's house and have a drink."

"Please, Tom, do you have to drink? Hasn't it done enough damage?"

"Listen up, you two drive me to drink. That is the reason I lost my job and our home."

"Don't put that on me and especially your daughter!"

Tom is getting more and more upset, and as soon as his wife begins to utter something else, he slaps her in the face. Mary grabs her face with her hand and quietly stares out the window whimpering. Vickie is sitting there with her mouth open as the tears build in her eyes. She knows not to cry or say anything as this will just draw her dad's anger to her. She is young but can sense the pain in her mom. The emotional tether is like an invisible connection of energy, a conduit of empathy flowing to and from them both. Hours pass and silence is king as the air is thick with control from Tom. He is on edge, unsure of what their future holds. He knows his older brother has always been there for him. Dan has always tried to take care of Tom growing up. Dan, in poor health, himself is happy to try to help especially since the death of his wife and son Derek moved out. Dan's home is quiet and inviting. Tom knows it is his safety net and a new start that may solve his problems. However, Tom does not know how to quiet the rage in him and can't even remember when it started. He sometimes thinks and wonders why he is so rough on Mary. It bothers him sometimes but the rage blinds him the other times. He is jittery, wanting his liquid courage.

Mary stares out the car window acting as if she has fallen asleep. But she can't sleep not knowing when the next rage or hit will come from Tom. Her instincts are to care for Vickie, and take the brunt of Tom's rage is her job now. Like a movie repeating itself, she thinks back to when Tom was so nice and caring when they dated. He was so handsome and a pure gentleman. The envy of her friends and she was so proud. Their marriage was beautiful and first year so perfect. She was pregnant after the first year and Tom was such a proud daddy. After the death of his dad and mom in a home invasion, it left him cold and troubled. Mary tried and tried to bring back the peace and caring of days past but Tom was stuck in a loop of self-pity and remorse. He never quite forgave himself for things he did growing up. His parents went through a lot to bring him around. He was always in trouble as a youth. It seemed like after they were gone, the restraint was broken on him. Mary has analyzed a million times trying to find the solution. None seem to be found, especially when she is hitting a brick wall with Tom. He is impenetrable and not interested in anymore kids. She has suggested before maybe he would be happier without her and Vickie but that was not an option for Tom. Maybe they are his only tie to bind him to normalcy but the struggle remains. His soul tormented by life and his traps. Mary just opens her eyes once in a while to make sure they are going the right way but does not dare to get Tom's attention. Her ears intently listen to Vickie playing quietly in the backseat. Vickie knows to stay quiet.

Vickie lives in her own little world far away from the harshness of her dad. She loves him so much and can even remember times he made her feel like a princess of a wonderful kingdom. He read to her and took her to parks constantly. She was the center of his universe. She does not understand what changed but only understands as her mom explained that daddy is sick. She prays every night that God will make him better. Vickie's emotional tie to Tom is severed now unlike with her mom. She can't afford to share the emotions of her dad. Like an instinct to protect children programmed genetically that protects little Vickie. Vickie is oblivious to the dynamics; she just knows her imagination is her refuge where she can build on the good memories to create fake ones. It is her fuel to keep going. She knows that someday her dad will come back to being healthy. That happy day will come soon. She patiently waits for the world to become happy again so she can pretend other things like about space. She loves anything to do with space and wants to grow up to be an astronomer. But that dream is on hold while she concentrates her focus on dad's health. Maybe when he is better, he will buy her another telescope to replace the one he broke in anger. She hopes and she dreams.

Home Away From Home

Tom, Mary, and Vickie arrive at Dan's house, and he comes out to greet them with open arms. "Tom, my little brother, it is so good to see you," Dan states. Dan turns to Mary. "Mary, so beautiful as before." He notices the red side of her face where she was struck earlier and asks, "Are you okay?"

Mary replies, "I am fine, I slept on it most of the way, what long trip."

Dan has a strange look and looks at Tom as Tom is unloading the car. Vickie runs up and Dan says, "Hey, pumpkin, you are getting so big!"

Vickie said, "Hi uncle."

Dan asked, "Are you hungry, Vickie?"

She nods yes, and he says, "Well, go in the kitchen and make yourself at home. I bought some snacks sitting on the counter just for you."

Vickie's eyes light up and she turns to her mom as Mary says, "Go ahead, Vickie."

She runs into the house in anticipation of the bounty. Mary looks at Dan and says, "Thank you, brother, I think you just won her over. All this has been so hard on her."

Dan said, "Not just her, I suspect."

Mary replies, "All that matters is her."

"Right."

Mary smiles and says, "I better help Tom."

"Right again," as Dan and Mary start unloading the car with Tom.

Later that evening, they are all moved in as there was not much really to move. Tom takes the trailer to a local branch that he had rented it from. While away and Vickie watching TV, Dan asked Mary, "Everything is going to get better now you are all here. I will take care of you guys and help Tom be a good man again."

Mary said, "Tom means well, we just need to get back on our feet."

Dan replied, "It is more than that. Tom is not the same since our parents were killed. He needs to forgive himself."

"I know but hell if he will listen to me."

"I think between us, we can reach him."

Mary begins to weep. "I hope so because I don't know how much more I can take."

Dan reaches out to her. "Listen, it will get better."

Mary nods her head yes and smiles wiping her tears away. She squeezes Dan's hand in thanks and walks to Vickie to watch TV and hold her. Tom returns and as the car door slams, Mary turns the TV off and she and Vickie come to attention. Dan stares in horror realizing things are much worse than he even realized. Tom comes in the house and says, "We're all done. Hey, Dan, do you have any beers?"

Dan replies, "Sure, Tom, in the fridge."

Mary says, "Tom, everything is put away."

Tom replied, "I am sure it is. You are always good about getting things done." Tom gets a beer and sits on the couch.

Mary tells Vickie, "C'mon, sweetie, let's get you cleaned up and ready for bed."

As they walk by, Dan says, "Good night, little princess."

Vickie smiles back at Dan as Dan looks at Tom. Tom is busy drinking and not even paying attention to Mary or Vickie. Dan grabs a beer and sits down in his favorite easy chair. It is quiet as the guys stare at their beer, and Tom wanders his eyes around the room of pictures.

Tom started, "Hey, I remember that bike you have."

Dan smiles. "Had, is more like it."

"What happened to that hog?"

"Had to sell it to pay for Susan's medical costs."

"I am sorry I could not make it to her funeral."

"That is all right, you had your own things to contend with."

"Hey, maybe tomorrow we can visit her grave."

Dan smiles. "That would be nice. She would appreciate that."

"She is still here with you, isn't she?"

"Always, she was my whole life. It was my honor to live with her and enjoy every day with her."

"Yea, that is nice. What was it like, you know, her with her illness?"

Dan stares at the ground. "It was nice and pleasant before her illness. Seem like life was perfect. Then one day, she paid a bill twice. I was concerned but we just shrugged it off as a senior moment even though we were not seniors. Then she got lost coming home and I had to go find her. Before we knew it, she could not remember simple things. Then she began to ask about wanting to see friends we have not known for years. She even mentioned wanting to watch you play basketball in high school."

Tom says, "Oh, brother, that is rough."

Dan looks up. "Yea, yea it was. I refused to put her in an Alzheimer's unit even though sometimes she did not recognize me. One time she thought I was our dad. Then all the sudden one morning I turned over to wake her and she was gone. She had a heart attack in her sleep. She looked so peaceful, you know. At peace finally, not agitated by her condition."

"How did Derek take it?"

"He was in college and kept coming back and forth to help. He was really good, a rock, solid. After his mom passed, he was more a comfort to me than I was to him. He is definitely his mother. She was always taking care of me, now he does."

"Where is he now?"

Dan replies, "Oh, does not live far from here. He should be stopping by tomorrow to see you guys. He is married to a woman named Sherry, and they have a son, thirteen months old."

"Wow, I have been gone too long."

"Well, you are here now and I think this is a blessing for all of us."

Tom replies sarcastically, "Yea, blessing."

"You know, Tom, you need to use the bad as much as the good. It is what makes us what we are."

"I know what you are saying but I don't need a sermon right now."

"Right, you just relax and focus on that wonderful wife and kid of yours. Your daughter is so beautiful."

Tom puts his beer on the table and asks, "Did you ever feel like your wife and kid were doing things to drive you crazy?"

Dan laughs. "I think we all go through that. I know hard times can skew our perception. What I have learned is that your spouse and kid are cogs in the machine. They move in the direction you do because they love you. Sometimes they trip over themselves trying too hard to please you. Remember, the tighter you grip sand, the more it slips out your grasp. You have to learn to cup your hands and gently hold the sand to keep all of it. Let them live and empower them to do what they know to do. You will find things happen automatically, and your life is so less stressful in the process."

Tom stares for a while at Dan and picks up his beer to drink. "If it only worked that way for me." Dan smirks as Tom finishes his beer and stands up. "Thank you, brother, for taking us in. I will find a job and be out of your hair as soon as possible."

Dan stands up and hugs Tom. "Tom, no rush, just relax. We have plenty of food and money here. Get better and get your family whole. You guys are welcome here for as long as you want or even permanently."

Tom smiles and goes to the bedroom to shower up. Mary and Vickie are already asleep. Tom stares at them both and with a troubled look goes to prepare for sleep.

The Grass is Meaner on the Other Side

Tom, Mary, and Vickie wake to the smell of bacon in the air. They wander into the kitchen and Dan has a spread of breakfast laid out for them.

Dan says, "Good morning, guys!"

Mary replied, "Oh my God, Dan, I would have made breakfast."

"You guys are still recuperating from your trip, besides it has been a while since I got to make breakfast for people. I love cooking, and you guys better get used to being catered to."

Tom smiles. "Okay, brother, you win, this looks great."

They all sit down as Dan dishes out eggs, bacons, and pancakes.

Vickie exclaims, "Pancakes!"

Dan smiles and says, "Here is some real maple syrup, cutie."

Vickie smiles at Mary with happiness as it has been a long time since she has had such a breakfast. Mary smiles back with pride. Tom is in his own world chomping bacon as if it was the last pig left on earth. Dan sits down and shares the moment.

Mary says, "Dan, thank you for everything."

Dan smiles. "Thank you for being here with me. This home needs a family again."

After breakfast everyone goes to get cleaned up and dressed for the day. Dan catches Tom alone. "Tom, how are you doing on funds?"

Tom sighs. "We have a couple of hundred left."

Dan hands him an envelope. Tom asks what is in the envelope and then opens it to find five thousand in hundreds.

"Dan, I can't take this."

"I have plenty of money from Susan's insurance, plus my pension. Look, I am twenty-three years older than you. I am not a young man anymore and have lived my life. I have money, you need it, take it, for your family's sake. Get clothes, whatever you need. If you need more, I have it."

Tom draws some tears and hugs his brother. "I love you, brother."

"Just take care of those two precious women, okay?"

Tom smiles at Dan and walks away.

Derek, the son of Dan, arrives with his wife Sherry and son Albert that afternoon. Hugs go all around as Dan introduces Derek and family to Tom's.

Tom told Derek, "You were just a kid the last time I saw you and look at you now, nephew."

Derek replies, "Hi, Uncle, it is good to see you after all this time. Say, you like to play golf?"

"It is been ages but I do miss it."

"Let me take to a cool course next week."

Tom smiles. "Sounds good."

Derek looks down and sees Vickie. He kneels down and asks, "You must be Vickie? I am your cousin Derek. You are such a pretty girl. How old are you?"

Vickie shy and looking away says, "Eight."

"Well, my son Albert is one and I think you two are going to be fun cousins."

"I thought we were cousins."

Derek laughs. "Yes, Albert is your second cousin."

Derek stands up and vigorously messes Vickie's hair and says to Mary, "She is adorable."

Mary replies, "So is your son. We just have a very pretty family, I guess."

Derek laughs. "Absolutely."

Mary looks over and Tom is giving her the evil eye; she stops smiling and looks away as if she has something else to do. Dan sees the interaction and starts to tell everyone, "Well, everyone sit down and let me get you all some tea."

Everyone sits as Dan goes to bring teas.

Derek asks Tom, "So was it a long trip?"

"It took a couple of days, had to sleep in our car halfway through. We got lost at one point and stopped in an abandoned old town called Destiny. Only thing there was an old gas station and someone still running it. Strangely it did not seem he had any gas to sell or anything else for that matter."

Sherry responds, "That is odd, guess he just could not let go to being there."

Mary says, "That is what it seemed. He said something strange to Vickie. Something about she would be important someday and influence many. I don't know, it really bothered me."

Tom replies, "Yea, those people out there by themselves turn feral after a while."

Sherry says, "Oh, Tom, you are so bad."

Tom and Derek laugh as the two seem to get along well.

Derek says, "Looks like you guys settled in fast for just getting here last night. Dad told me you had a trailer."

Tom replies, "That's right, we rented and packed it full. Fact is, we sold a lot of things before coming down so we could afford to move. I lost my job at the factory and our savings just could not hold us long."

Sherry says, "I am so sorry to hear about that."

Tom replies, "Yea, us too. I was at that factory for ten years. My dad got me a job there. Can't believe he had just retired after forty years when he and mom were killed."

Derek looking at Tom and Dan in the kitchen. "Did they ever catch the men that did that?"

Tom stares intently and says, "No, they never did." Quietly to himself says, "And they never will."

The room draws quiet as Dan breaks in as a fresh air. "Here are the teas." Everyone refreshes themselves as Derek says to Dan, "Tom was just telling us about grandma and grandpa."

Dan says, "Yes, what a horrible event. Mom and dad were set to go cruising all the time. They went once before and saved their pennies to go often in retirement."

Derek says, "They must have had a nice savings for you guys when they passed."

Tom replies, "We both got something but it did not last long with us."

Mary looks away in disgust as she watches Vickie playing on the floor with a golf and tennis ball as if they are planets.

Derek looks down at Vickie and says, "Mary, what is she playing?"

Mary replies, "She loves astronomy and wants to be a scientist."

Vickie says, "My telescope broke."

Derek says, "Well you know what, Vickie? I have a really cool telescope and you are welcome to see it anytime."

Vickie's face lights up and she looks at Mary. Mary smiles at Vickie as Vickie goes back to playing planets.

The evening draws to a close as Derek and Tom walk down the sidewalk having a couple of beers.

Derek asks, "Tom, you like guns?"

Tom replies, "I used to have a nice pistol but had to sell it."

"I have a couple of decent pistols and a shotgun. We should go to the range and blow something up."

"Derek, thanks for making me feel really welcome here."

"I can only imagine what you guys have been through. We are family, we are in it together." Tom has a feeling of friendship with Derek and identifies with him. Derek and his family leave at the end of the evening meal prepared by Dan. Mary and Dan clean up as Tom comes in and grabs another beer and sits in front of the TV.

Mary tells Dan, "I wish he would not drink so much."

Dan says, "I notice he drinks like a fish."

They continue washing, and after a few minutes, Dan asks, "Mary, can I ask you a personal question?"

Mary replies, "Sure."

"Does Tom hit you?"

Mary washes not looking up as Dan stops and stares at her. Mary looks up at Dan and smiles and looks down again. She then stops for a brief moment and says, "Sometimes."

"How about Vickie?"

Mary looks toward the living room at Vickie sitting on the couch next to her dad, "Fortunately no."

Dan continues washing. "That is not right."

"Please don't mention it to him."

"No, I won't of course."

They dry the plates as Dan stares at Tom drinking his beer. Later that night, Tom and Mary put Vickie to bed and she drifts off to sleep dreaming of planets and stars. Mary smiles looking at Vickie's face asleep as Tom is standing near. Mary looks back at Tom with a smile that soon escapes. Tom looks at Vickie and back at Mary and then slaps Mary hard. Mary's eyes are rolling with tears as she asks, "Why did you hit me?"

Tom replies, "You just had to be a bit of a smart ass to Derek and his family tonight, didn't you? And I thought you told Vickie not to mention anything about her telescope or the other toys."

Mary nods her head yes. "It was my mistake, I am so sorry. Please don't take it out on Vickie."

Tom sneers at Mary as she covers Vickie with her body. Tom rolls into bed where he promptly passes out. Mary goes into the bathroom and puts her face in a towel to cry.

Bearing Arms at Close Range

DEREK AND TOM decide to go to the gun store to replace Tom's gun and shoot some. As they come home, Derek says, "That is a nice forty-five pistol you have there.

Tom replies, "Yea, it is a 1911 style like my dad had. Good shooting gun."

"Pistols are nice but for home invasion, you need a shotgun."

Tom laughs. "I will do just fine with my pistol."

"Just saying, nothing stops the fight like a shotgun."

The two return to Dan's house as Derek drops Tom off. Tom comes in and shows Mary and Dan his new pistol. They are obviously concerned as Dan asks, "That is a beauty. Did you get a lock for it?"

Tom looks at him with a smile. "Don't need a lock, Vickie knows not to mess with my stuff."

Dan replies, "I am not worried about Vickie but worried about some other kid that visits. Vickie will have friends when she starts school. Look for my peace of mind, put a lock on it."

"Fine. I will get a lock tomorrow."

"Thank you."

Dan leaves to his room as Mary stares at Tom. Vickie is playing only momentarily distracted by the cold black gun. Tom smiles at Mary and briefly aims it at her.

Mary's eyes get big and says, "Tom!"

He interrupts her quickly, "Hey, it was just a joke. Besides, it is unloaded."

"Every gun is loaded even unloaded ones. Even I know that."

"Whatever."

Tom leaves it on the couch and gets a beer.

"Ah please put that away if you are going to drink."

Tom pops the beer can open. "What's the matter, you afraid I am going to go mad on you?"

"I am just saying have some sense, alcohol makes you forgetful and careless and with a dangerous weapon, something will happen."

Tom is about to take a drink and sets the can down on the table. "Fine."

Tom picks the gun up and says, "Vickie, come here."

Mary reacts, "Tom."

Tom gestures her to shut up.

Vickie comes over and says, "That is a pretty gun, Daddy."

"Yes it is and it is for our protection. You don't ever get near it, understand?"

Vickie nods yes.

"If you ever see anyone near it, you stop them, understand?"

Vickie nods and says, "Yes, Daddy."

Tom asks, "You want to hold it, kiddo?"

Mary shouts, "Tom!"

"Fine, okay. Vickie, get back to playing."

"Okay, Daddy." Vickie returns to her game as Tom stares at his blue steel glory. Mary just stares in disdain. Tom packs the gun off to the bedroom to hide it and comes back to finish his beer.

My Brother My Keeper

IT HAS BEEN over a year and Tom has been working at a local manufacturer, but he and his family have settled as their home with his brother Dan. Mary has mastered the art of hiding Tom's abuse so to not get Dan's involvement. But Tom working has made a marked improvement in his temper but the drinking stays the same. Mary notices that Dan has been getting tired more quickly than normal as she asks, "Dan, are you okay?"

Dan responds, "I have pains in my shoulder blades once in a while and my chest stings once in a while. I just can't seem to catch my breath at times."

"We need to get you to a doctor."

"No, I am fine, this has happened a couple of years ago but went away."

"Please go see a doctor. If something happened to you it would be devastating to us."

Dan smiles. "Mary, you have nothing to worry about. If something did, you guys would be able to stay in this house for as long as you like even though Derek would inherit it."

"That is not what I am talking about. I need you to be well."

"I know what you mean. I will be all right."

Summer has arrived and Dan's health seems to get weaker but refused to get it checked out. Tom, Dan, and Mary are sitting around the living room talking about a variety of subjects as they do many times. The room seems festive as Tom tells old stories to Dan.

Tom says, "There was one time Mary got some virus and she was like a drunk all week. She would stare at the walls like a zombie."

Dan asks, "Mary, what kind of virus was that?"

Mary looks around. "It is called the Xanax virus."

The room gets quiet and Dan asks, "Xanax as in the pill?"

Mary nods yes.

Tom looks shocked and quiet.

Dan asks, "Why did you need to take Xanax?"

Mary looks at Tom and says, "I was going through some stress at the time."

Tom cuts in with, "That was the time you had lost your aunt and had a hard time dealing with it, remember?"

Mary looks back at Tom. "No, it was after the time you hit me so hard it knocked me out."

Tom gasps and looks over at Dan. Dan looks at the ground. "Tom why are you hitting Mary?"

Tom refuses to answer, as Mary answers, "I did not put the cap on the motor oil tight enough and it fell over spilling down the garage."

Tom stares at the floor.

Dan says, "What the hell is wrong with you, Tom! Is it because mom and dad were killed you have to take it out on Mary and Vickie?"

Tom exclaims, "I never hit Vickie!"

"You don't have to brother. You don't think she feels what you do to her mommy?"

Tom says, "I don't know what gets into me. I just get so furious that I don't even think rationally anymore."

Dan replies, "You need to stop drinking. Stop making it your coping mechanism."

"I can stop anytime I want. I just need it to take the edge of things."

"That means you are using it as behavioral medication, which means you are not dealing with the real problem."

Tom breaks down crying. "I had a big fight with mom and dad just before they were killed."

Dan looks over at Mary as Mary begins to tear up. Dan says, "That's it, Tom, let it out."

Tom puts his face in his hands and then stares at the floor some more. "I was such a disappointment to them.

Dad went out on a limb and got me a job but I kept messing up. I had so many chances because of dad and his good standing with the company."

Mary slowly gets up and smiles to Dan as she goes to the bedroom to check on Vickie and leave the two brothers alone. Tom is in his own world confessing all the issues of his past. Dan explains that he had many talks with their dad.

"Tom, Dad was always proud of you. He knew you had to try harder than I because of your personal demons. He admired how you kept trying."

It seemed like a huge weight lifted off Tom. Tom is speechless as Dan nods okay. The brothers embrace as Tom goes to his bedroom. Vickie is asleep as Mary looks at Tom, and he sits next to her.

Tom says, "I am so sorry for everything. I have been so horrible to you. I am going to be better."

Mary rolls some tears and says, "It will be all right." Mary has heard it before though. Tom smiles as they go to bed.

Tom, Mary, and Vickie go off on a mini-vacation for a week; the first vacation they have had in years. They have a great time traveling and seeing the sights. It is like a perfect vacation and Tom has drunk very little. When they return, Mary calls out to Dan but receives no reply. She knocks on his bedroom door and sees him lying on the bed with a book on his chest.

She checks, "Dan?" She shakes him but no response and he is stiff as a board. She begins crying and yells out to Tom. Tom comes in smiling and Mary looks at Tom while standing next to Dan. The smile leaves Tom's face as shock sets in. Tom stands over Dan and says in a terrible cry, "No. Not you." Tom mumbles, "I have no one now."

Mary says, "Honey, we are still here." Tom looks up with his face red and eyes watered, and then puts his head down on Dan's body crying excessively.

The funeral was attended by Tom and Derek's family as well as numerous townspeople. Dan was well liked as he had apparently died from a heart attack. They all stare as the preacher gives Scriptures and final words. Vickie stares crying as her uncle's casket is lowered. He was like the grandpa she never got to experience.

Derek tells Tom, "The house is yours to live as long as you want."

Tom thanks him.

Derek says, "It is what dad wanted."

They leave as if chains that kept stability in everyone's lives were broken. Tom who had been clean and sober for almost a year picks up beers. Mary says nothing as she lets him grieve in his own way.

Weeks pass as Tom's drinking continues and becomes the norm again. Their happy peace is deteriorating since Dan's death.

Mary tells Tom, "Tom please stop drinking and let us get back to health like before."

Tom stands up and says, "You knew Dan was having issues and you did not talk him into getting checked out by a doctor."

Mary starts crying. "I tried to talk him into it long ago but he would not listen to me."

"Bullshit! He loved you and would do whatever you asked."

"What are you talking about?"

"You apply your siren-like seduction to make my brother do what you want."

"What?"

"That's right. You knew he was weak willed from losing his wife. I could see you guys whispering all the time together."

"Tom, he was asking me about you hitting me. I asked him not get involved but he constantly asked me. He knew every time you did something to me."

"Hmmm, that is interesting, and how many times did you sleep with him, whore?"

"Don't you call me that!"

Tom slaps Mary to the floor as she holds her face crying with a bloody nose. Mary stands up and runs to the bedroom as Tom chases her. They both come in and see Vickie holding Tom's gun and aiming it at her dad. Mary slowly walks over to Vickie and says, "Honey, let me have the gun." The gun has a lock on the trigger but Vickie shakes holding it crying. "Daddy, stop hurting mommy!" Tom sees this mess he has created and it hits him like a brick wall. He seems like he is standing outside himself seeing all them in a movie and drops to the corner of the room weeping bitterly. Mary gently takes the gun away from Vickie as she hugs Mary crying.

Vickie asks, "Why won't Daddy stop?"

Mary responds, "Quiet now, baby, you stopped him. You stopped him."

Treaties and Treatment

TOM ENTERS AN alcoholic treatment program and gets half pay leave from his company. Meanwhile, Mary and Vickie are often visited by Derek and Sherry. Derek more and more becomes the virtual dad that Vickie needs. Life is somewhat peaceful but Vickie has a deep hole missing her dad but fearful of him too. She has become more reasoning of the issues she has quickly had to grow up to understand. Tom spends his time in a facility that is like a hotel where people watch you constantly and test your urine. He goes to activities they have to help reinforce positive ways to deal with stress and then the evenings are with groups where they share and go over concepts of sobriety. At first, he laughs it off and does not understand why he really needs to be there because the rest of the patients are really messed up. Over the weeks, he realized he was just as messed up and need help. In his fifth week, the spouses of those in treatment are brought in to share their pain with them. Tom sits on his hands as he hears the crying and anger of those venting to their loved ones. Finally, it is Mary's turn. She stands and stares at Tom as the tension grows.

Mary starts, "The first time you hit me, I felt shock and disbelief that it actually happened. Like it was an accident or something. I ignored it as later it happened again. I began to get rid of a beer or two once in a while so you would have less to drink. But that failed as you simply spent more of our money to get more. I was always worried you would hurt Vickie. After a while I took medication for depression." Mary looks around a bit but looks back at Tom. "I hated it when you drank. Every time you hit me I felt I could kill you. Eventually, I quit hating the drink and hated you." Mary cries in anger. "I hated you!"

She sits down as another spouse hands her a tissue. Tom looks at the ground as the counselor asks Tom if he would like to respond. Tom shakes his head no looking at the ground. Mary leaves with other spouses and Tom makes way to his room to process what was said. He is taught how to deal with life issues and to forgive himself. The treatment breaks him down from his rock bottom despair to a moment of clarity. The last week has been hell for him but also a renewal. He feels clearer than he ever has before. Before he leaves, his counselor asks him, "Tom, what is the future going to be like for you?"

Tom replies, "I have a lot of repairs to make. I have a lot to atone for. I know it will be much better."

The counselor tells him, "Remember, there are things greater than alcohol. Whenever it feels like alcohol is the biggest thing, it is not. Go to meetings, avoid things that trigger you."

"Thank you for giving me my life back."

"You are welcome. Just remember that alcoholism is not cured, only maintained."

Returning home, his wife and daughter are excited but hesitant. Derek and his family are with them to make sure things go smoothly. Tom arrives home from the cab and takes a deep breath. As he walks in the door, they all stare at him in silence. He puts his luggage down and says, "Hi, honey, I'm home."

Mary runs to him and hugs him tightly crying. She looks back and Vickie is staring at them. "Sweetie, don't you want to hug your daddy?"

Tom kneels down and says, "Daddy did a lot of things he can't take back, but I love you and want to make it all better."

Vickie looks up at mommy and Mary nods her head toward to Tom. Vickie looks back at her daddy and slowly walks toward him. She stops in front of him as Tom has tears running down his cheeks. Vickie stares at him with a deadpan stare and then busts out crying, grabbing him saying, "Daddy!"

The emotions are contagious causing even Derek and Sherry to tear up. Derek and Sherry walk over and Tom hugs them holding Vickie in his arm.

Derek says, "So good to see you, Tom."

"Thank you for taking care of my family."

"Of course, how could we not. Especially with that cute little girl you have."

Vickie turns shy and embarrassed by Derek's comment. Mary happily cries as it has been a while since she has seen the shy Vickie.

A Fire Grows

TIME PASSES AND Vickie is twelve now. Tom, for the most part, has been a good husband and father. He casually drinks and, once in a great while, argues with Mary. But she gives as good as she gets and the violence has ceased. Tom sees his drinking sponsor when things get out of control. Sometimes when things are at its worse, Vickie will spend a week or two over Derek's. It gives her the sanctuary that she needs so desperately. Derek remains like a father figure as Vickie has developed strong feelings for him. He spends time talking to her, and he is about the only one outside her mom that she can trust. Once in a while, she will spend the night at Derek's in order to use the telescope he has. He never lets her borrow it or have it because then there would be no need for her to spend nights. But Vickie does not mind, his house and family are so much more peaceful than hers. She looks at the stars and dreams of a future studying them. Derek often talks to her and expounds his wisdom of age to her. He is patient, caring, and enjoys the adoration Vickie has for him.

Vickie talks to her mom while Mary is folding clothes, "Mom, can I ask you a question about boys?"

Mary responds, "You are thirteen, I knew this day would come."

"Why do they act like they are not interested in you?"

Mary laughs. "Because they are. It is their ego that does that. They act like they are not interested to be cool with their friends. It also makes you pursue them."

"I thought it was because I have really high grades in school."

"Yea, brainy girls tend to bother guys sometimes. But some really like them. Is there one you like? Bet it is that Brian boy, isn't it?"

"Mom! Brian is okay but Todd is cuter."

"Todd, is that the boy that likes soccer so much?"

"No, that is Brian, Todd is the basketball guy."

"Oh I see."

Vickie stares at the clothes.

"Why don't you introduce yourself to Todd."

"I don't know. He is kind of a wimp."

"Wimp? That is not nice, Vickie."

"I like him and I don't know why. But the bullies pick on him."

"I think you feel sorry for him and want to protect him."

"Maybe."

The next day Mary gets a call to school that Vickie is in trouble. Mary arrives and the disciplinary principal has Vickie wait outside his office while he talks to her mom. The principal says, "Mrs. Newsome, Vickie violated the honor code here at school by harming another kid."

Mary responds, "Oh my, what did she do?"

"It seems the boy she harmed was bullying another boy. Now the bully was told to leave him alone. Vickie later did something to the bully."

"What did she do?"

"The boy fell asleep in class on his desk. She managed to glue his face down to the desk."

Mary tries to keep a straight face. "I'm sorry. I will talk with her."

"She will be suspended for a few days."

"I understand. Is the boy okay?"

"Yes, the glue is water based so it was not hard to free him. But something a bit more to it though."

"What is that?"

"One of the kids overheard Vickie whispering something to the boy when he came to and started to panic about being stuck to the desk. She said something to the affect that if he ever bothers Todd again, she would make the glue permanent next time."

"Oh my."

"We are concerned that your daughter may have some sociopathic issues. Maybe she should be seeing a counselor when she comes back to school."

"Is that necessary? Obviously, she was protecting a boy that was being tormented. She does not like bullies."

"But she has become the bully herself."

"I understand that and I will deal with her. But from her perspective, nothing was stopping the bully from her friend. Have we addressed that issue?"

"Look, we are doing the best we can with the resources we have. There is a limited number of us and over a thousand of them."

"This is not a prison. They are children for God's sakes. The day you quit treating them like that is the day they will quit acting as children." Mary gets up and signs the paper of the incident. She goes outside the office. "Come on, Vickie."

The principal stands at the door as Vickie looks back at him. On the drive home, Mary says, "You are out of school for three days. I am going to tell your dad you are sick, understand?"

Vickie replies, "Understand."

"Now tell me why in God's name you glued that boy to the desk?"

Vickie stares out the window.

"Well?"

"I don't know, Mom. I just got tired of him picking on Todd."

"What are you going to do when the bully gets back at you?"

"That would be a bad mistake."

"Excuse me, little miss?"

"Mom, he needed to be taught a lesson."

"Are you the facilitator of such punishments?"

Vickie rolls her eyes around.

"Well, are you?"

"No!"

"Watch your tone."

"Sorry."

Mary calms down and grabs Vickie's hand briefly. "Honey, you can't do these things. I know this comes from how your dad has been. I know somehow you want to protect people. I get it."

Vickie looks at Mary. "I will never let anyone do to me what dad did to you."

Mary looks at Vickie and sees a look of seriousness and concentration she has never seen before. She continues to drive on as no more conversation is made.

Vickie returns to school and it seems everyone wants to be her friend. The bully walks by her in the hallway with an evil eye.

Vickie chimes, "Remember what I said."

The bully's eyes grow large and he walks faster.

Todd walks up to Vickie, "Hi, Vickie."

Vickie replies, "Hi, Todd."

"Sorry you got suspended."

"Not sure why *not* going to school is considered a punishment."

"Is kind of funny. Hey, you think I can come over to your house and we play something?"

"I am not allowed visitors at home."

"Oh well maybe you can come over."

"My dad only allows me to hang out with my cousin. But maybe my mom can visit the local park and meet there sometime."

"Awesome!"

"See you in class."

Todd has a big smile on his face as he leaves. Vickie sits in class as the teacher talks and writes notes on the blackboard. She notices the bully is staring at her.

Vickie says, "Don't fall asleep."

The bully looks angry as Todd is grinning. A couple of days pass and Vickie is upset coming from school.

Mary asks, "What is wrong, dear?"

Vickie replies, "Todd told me that his mother is not allowing him to be around me anymore. He said she is afraid that I am a bad influence."

Mary stokes Vickie's hair. "Well, there are other kids to be friends with. I'm sorry, sweetie." Mary comforts her but suspects that the mother of the bully has talked with the mother of Todd. She feels maybe it is for the better because now Vickie no longer has to protect him anymore.

The Trap

A S THE YEARS pass, he can sense her feelings for him as he lets nature make her more mature. Vickie's parents have a big fight and Vickie stays over Derek's for another weeklong excursion. Vickie is upset so Derek takes her in his car to drive a little reckless. It distracts her from the pain for a while. It seems nothing is like spinning out tires to get the adrenaline pumping. Toward the evening, Derek takes her to a walk through the park.

Vickie says, "I'm sixteen and this is supposed to be a happy time of my life, but my parents just fight all the time."

Derek smiles and nods his head yes listening to her.

Vickie continues, "I never see you fight with Sherry."

Derek responds, "Oh we fight. We just try not air our dirty laundry in public. Look, I know it has been tough on you living with that. However you are strong, I can sense it. You have an amazing way to turning things to your advantage. You are smart and crafty. I have seen you manipulate your dad, and your mom has told me about a few other times you outsmarted him."

Vickie blushes and smiles. "Survival techniques, I guess. It is kind of funny but I really do not enjoy treating my dad that way. Deep down inside, he is a wonderful man but there is just something he can't get past. When your dad was around, my dad seemed to control himself better."

Derek looks at her and nods yes. "My dad was much like a father to your dad. Sometimes, being the eldest brother plays that role. They feel like they have to step in for their father and assume responsibility."

"Kind of like what you do for me."

"Maybe. I like to think of you more like a good friend." Derek suggests they sit down and enjoy the view on a small hill overlooking the town. "Can I share something personal with you, Vickie?"

"Sure, cousin, anything."

"Sometimes I wish things were different. Sometimes I wish you were not my cousin and we were closer to the same age because I would definitely date a girl like you."

Vickie blushes and astonished at the revelation and starts to become shy. "Derek, I love you and if we're not related, I would surely date you but we are."

"You did not mention anything about age?"

"Age does not matter to me."

They smile and laugh for a bit until the smiles leave and Derek kisses Vickie. Vickie is taken by the kiss for a short time but pulls away. "I am sorry!"

"It is okay."

Vickie smiles as Derek tries to kiss her again but she pulls away pushing him away. Vickie says, "No…please."

Derek withdraws. "I am sorry, Vickie, you are so beautiful. I don't know what got over me."

Vickie looks around a little shaken but calms down. "It is okay, I understand."

They get up and Derek says, "Come on, let's go home and have something cool to drink. Let us just forget about this okay?"

Vickie smiles. "Okay."

The drive home is quiet, nothing said, and they enter the house as Vickie sits on the couch to watch TV. Sherry asks how is everyone doing and almost in harmony both Vickie and Derek respond, "Great." They both look at each other. The house is quiet for a couple of days while both Derek and Vickie seem to avoid each other. Then Sherry took the kids to her parents for small reunion of certain family members of hers. They would be gone all day, and as she left the house was quiet. Vickie is reading a book, and he goes back and forth between rooms looking at her. Finally, he says, "Vickie, would you like a game of chess?"

Vickie replies, "I would love it, cousin."

With the tension broken, Derek says, "Okay, set the table up and I will get us a couple of sodas."

"Awesome." Vickie sets up the chess table, and Derek brings a couple of cans of soda to the living room table.

Derek places an open can of soda next to Vickie and opens his can. "Here you go. Now who goes first?"

"You better go first, that way you will lose slower this time."

Derek smiles. "Oh I see, just because you won every game we have played so far, you think you will win again."

"Just going by statistics, cousin, it is a mathematical probability."

The game progresses as they drink their sodas, and Vickie is already taking pieces from Derek as if it is effortless.

Vickie says, "You don't seem bothered this time when I am taking your men?"

Derek replies, "I am getting used to it."

"Well, you should be used to it by..." Vickie shakes her head and feels her forehead.

"What is wrong, Vickie?"

Vickie mumbles and her eyes are sluggish, "I feel dizzy."

Vickie falls over as Derek grabs her. He lays her gently on the floor and grabs the can of soda she was drinking and sniffs it. He then takes the soda into the kitchen and pours it out in the sink and washes it out with sink water. Then he throws the can out and gets another cold soda, opens it and pours half into the sink. He walks over to the living room table and lifts Vickie up pressing her lips against the soda can as if she was drinking it and lays the can on the table. He then puts towels on her bed and comes back to place her on the bed directly over the towels. Derek steps back to stare at Vickie then checks the house and outside to make sure everything is calm. He approaches her bedroom unbuttoning his shirt as he closes her door.

Vickie wakes up groggy and sees Derek sitting on the side of her bed.

Derek says, "Relax, you passed out. The doctor said you need to rest."

Vickie asks, "Where is the doctor?"

"I called him and he told what to do. He said there is a lot of pollen that is affecting people. You must have an allergy. Just rest and I will get you some water."

Derek gets up and goes to the kitchen. Vickie looks at the clock and sees hours that have passed. He comes back in with water and says, "Drink lots of water to get that nasty pollen out your system." Vickie drinks and thanks him. Derek smiles and gets up. "I am going to the living room, just yell if you need something." Vickie continues to drink but as she starts to come out the sleepy fog in her head, a pain begins to reveal itself. She is feeling sting in her groin that grows more painful as she gains more of herself back. She is certain that her clothes are not right. They are where they are supposed to be but something is just not right about them. Her shoes are tied differently than the way she does it. After a few minutes, she wonders to her bathroom and checks herself out for the pain. Her groin is red as if was scrubbed but she notices something else and tears start to pour out her eyes as she realizes what has happened. She whimpers quietly as the horrible prospect of what she knows in her heart has happened. Confused and scared, she jumps as Derek knocks on the door. "Are you are all right, cousin?"

Vickie replies, "I am fine, just this pollen has my eyes watering and a head cold. But everything else is just fine."

"Okay good."

Vickie stands up and looks at the mirror. She wipes her face dry and says to herself quietly, "Pull yourself together, Vickie. I need you to act normal like nothing happened." She manages to control the tears as she stares deeply into the mirror at herself. Something has changed in her; she no longer feels fear and sadness but something else. She leaves the bathroom and heads to the living where Derek is, he is watching TV.

"Are you okay, cousin?"

Vickie looks at him. "I am fine, cousin." Vickie sits down and starts putting the chessboard pieces back to a start position. "Say, how about finishing that game."

Derek looks around and smiles. "Okay."

Vickie picks up her number two soda can left there and she looks at it, then looks at Derek. Derek looks at both. Vickie can tell this is not the can from before and knows what he has done, she then drinks from it. Derek just stares at her. Vickie smiles at him. "Your move." Derek looks a little taken back and moves one of the chess pieces. As the game progresses, Vickie viciously defeats him.

Derek says, "Wow, you must be feeling better."

Vickie replies, "I feel awake."

Derek has a concerned look as Vickie is staring at him as if a new person is staring at him. At that time, Sherry and the kids walk in; "Hello, honey, hello, Vickie. I see you guys are playing chess again. I thought for sure you two were fighting."

Derek replies, "Oh no, just giving each other our space."

Vickie says, "We just needed some time to understand each other."

Derek looks at Vickie, "Yea, anyway how was the reunion, dear?"

Sherry begins to enthusiastically tell Derek all about who was there and what happened. Derek listens but once in a while he looks down at Vickie as he notices she is staring at him. After Sherry finishes and Derek takes one of his kids, Vickie stands up and comes over to him.

Vickie says, "I am not feeling well, can I go back home now."

Sherry answers, "Of course, dear. Derek will take you back."

"Sure let me get my keys."

Vickie looks at Sherry. "Well, you will have your home back tonight without me. I am sure Derek is anxious to impose himself on you as a man does."

Sherry responds, "Vickie! That is not nice, what has got into you?"

"Derek must have got into me."

Derek's face turns red and says, "Vickie! Let's get you home."

Vickie turns her head toward him with a smug look as Derek looks like a wet dog walking away to the car. Sherry looks at Vickie with disgust as Vickie winks at her and blows her a kiss. Sherry looks with a horrified face as Vickie walks to the car.

As they drive back, Derek breaks the silence and asks, "Are you okay, cousin?"

Vickie responds, "I am just fine, lover."

"Cousin, it is cousin."

"Whatever you say."

Derek begins to pull into her parents' driveway and says, "I hope you feel better from your illness."

Vickie looks at Derek. "I loved you."

Derek has a distraught look as Vickie leaves quickly to her house.

House of W-Horrors

Vickie walks through the front door, still feeling the pain of the whole event, both physically and mentally. She feels a sense of safety being away from Derek but knows she is just walking into another. Her parents obviously had been fighting recently as they are not talking. She tells her mom she is not feeling well and going to bed early. Her mom simply shrugs her off. Vickie lies in her bed thinking about the rape over and over like a car going in a circle, never parking. Then the suppression of feelings that dammed up herself so she could deal with Derek collapses and she starts to cry. She thinks, *What did I do that was so wrong to deserve this? How could he take advantage of me when I loved him? Did I lead him on? I hate myself and I don't want to live anymore?* She cries quietly for hours until exhaustion takes over and she falls asleep. She dreams of being unable to move while Derek is taking off her clothes and unable to scream until she jumps in bed waking up.

Her mom says, "Dear, you must have been having a nightmare. You slept in your clothes. I was trying to get them off you."

Vickie, "Mom, something terrible has happened."

"I know. Derek told me this morning that you almost wrecked his car while he was teaching you to drive, and you got some kind of sickness and slept it off."

Vickie nervously asks, "Is he here?"

"No, he called. He was concerned about you. He cares for you a great deal. Like a little sister he never had."

"I would not say sister."

"Silly. I know he is your cousin. Are you feeling better?"

"Mom, I need to tell you something but I don't know how to tell you."

Mary looks puzzled. "What, dear?"

Vickie ponders as her mind swirls with emotions like a meteor storm in her brain. "If someone hurt me badly, what would you do?"

"Did that boy last school year do something to you?"

"No, just what if."

"Vickie, don't worry about things that have not happened. We were thinking of having Derek and family over for dinner."

Vickie's eyes widen and she quickly replies, "No. I mean, I am not feeling well."

"Okay, just take it easy today." Mary gets up and begins to leave her room when Vickie asks, "Mom…"

"What, dear?"

Vickie looks down. "Never mind."

"You are a strange one. Get out of those old clothes and get cleaned up." Mary leaves and Vickie prepares for a shower. She is almost scared to take her clothes off but manages and gets in the shower. She scrubs and then scrubs obsessively but can never seem to get clean. After over an hour, she finally gets out the shower. She dries off and opens the bathroom door and looks at the bed, fear washes over her, and the room almost begins to swirl. After a few moments, it passed and she gets dressed. She comes out to the living room and her dad is gone. Vickie walks to the living couch and lies down. Her mom brings her a sandwich and glass of water. "Here you go, dear." Mary looks upon the wreck that is Vickie, just lying there staring off.

Mary, "Vickie, are you okay?"

Vickie is motionless.

"Eat your sandwich." Mary walks off in frustration. Mary grabs her things and tells Vickie she is running a couple of errands.

Vickie snaps out her catatonic state and says; "Mom, please don't leave!"

"What's wrong, Vickie?"

Vickie stares back and says, "Nothing."

"Well then I'll be right back."

Vickie lies back down adding a slight sense of fear as she is alone. She awakens to the sound of the door closing as her dad has come in. He turns the TV on and sits down his chair. "What is wrong with you?"

Vickie just stares aimlessly.

"Where is your mother?"

Vickie mumbles, "Errands."

"Late supper again. Aren't you going to eat your sandwich?"

Vickie replies, "Not hungry."

Tom gets up and goes to the kitchen to grab a beer and returns grabbing Vickie's sandwich. "Well if you're not going to eat it." He begins to eat and watch TV. Vickie simply lies on the couch with no real thoughts, just emptiness.

An hour later, Mary returns. "Vickie, are you still lying on that couch, well at least you ate your sandwich."

Vickie, "Dad ate it."

"Tom, that was for her."

Tom, "She wasn't eating it and I'm hungry."

"Well I brought home food from Antonio's, but I guess you can have tomorrow since you ate." Mary walks to the kitchen and Tom mumbles, "witch."

Vickie just stares at her dad as if she is a computer processing things. After a few minutes, Vickie asks her dad, "Dad, what would you do if someone raped me?"

Mary walks partially to the living listening in on the strange question. Tom stops looking at the TV and turns. "What the hell kind of question is that?"

"What would you do?"

"Listen, you don't need to be worrying about things like that. Besides, if that happen to you, I have a special place I would take the bastard."

Mary walks in. "Oh and what about me?"

Tom looks back at Mary. "You, I would send a thank you card to the rapist."

"Oh that is nice right in front of our daughter to say that to me."

Tom has a look of unconcern and watches TV again. Mary stands with her hands on her hips and mouth open. "I don't know why I stay with you, Tom. I really don't."

Tom, "Nothing is keeping you here."

Mary, "That is right, Tom, there is nothing keeping me here. Well, except the fact we have a daughter. Someday, I am going to have enough and we are going to leave you."

Tom looks around and then his anger hits as he stands up. "Look you, she is not going anywhere. You can leave anytime you want!" As the usual fight ensues, Vickie slowly gets up and walks to her room and closes the door. She lays in bed listening to the door-muffled sounds of her parents screaming at each other. She can hear them go through a laundry list of past issues that she has heard over and over. But she is in her own world now.

Weeks pass and Vickie has been unresponsive, barely eating, and even sick at times. Vickie lies in her bed looking at an astronomy book. Mary walks in and sits down next to her. "Vickie, you have been moping around for weeks now. Your dad does not seem to care but I do."

Vickie offers no response as she holds onto her book.

Mary, "Your favorite astronomy book, we need to see about getting you to be an astronomer. Only a couple of more years till you start on that career."

Vickie replies. "I don't want to be an astronomer anymore."

"Why not?"

"I hate it now."

"Well, we all change tastes, is that what is bothering you?"

"Part of it."

"You are nervous about what to be in life I bet. I was scared when I was your age. The big bad world was just around the corner. Your dad and I have made a terrible time of it for you." Vickie sits up and hugs her mom. "You know you can tell me anything."

"Anything?"

"Of course, anything."

Vickie looks up with tears rolling down her face. "Mom, I was raped."

Mary face shows a huge grimace. "What? How? When?"

Vickie swallows and says, "Cousin Derek drugged me the last time I was over there and then raped me." Vickie stares at the ground crying while her mom grabs her head.

"Tell me everything, Vickie."

"Sherry took their kids to a family reunion so it was just me and Derek. Derek took me in his car to do some driving lessons but we ended up racing his car around. It was a lot of fun. Then we went to a park and talked for the longest time. We sat and he kissed me. He tried again and I pushed him away. He apologized and we went back to his house. For a while, we did not speak but he convinced me to play a game of chess and brought some sodas. After drinking mine, I became dizzy and the next thing I know I was in bed with Derek sitting next to me. He told me I passed out and he had a glass of water. But I knew I had been drugged and raped."

Mary holding her hand over her mouth with tears in her eyes. "Oh my God. Why didn't you tell me then?"

"I tried, I couldn't."

"Let's go, we need to take you to a doctor to get checked out."

"I'm sorry, Mom."

"You have nothing to be sorry about, this happened to you. You did nothing wrong, understand?"

Vickie crying nods her head yes. "I love you, Mom."

Mary hugs Vickie. "I love you too. We will get past this."

Vickie and Mary have visited the doctor, and he confirmed she has been raped and is pregnant. As they drive home, Mary says, "We have to tell your father."

Vickie, "Please no."

"You are going to show eventually and it will be obvious soon. He needs to know now."

Vickie stares out the side window and is quiet all the way home. They arrive and Tom is already home watching

TV. Vickie sits down on the couch and Mary turns the TV off and sits on the couch beside Vickie.

Tom, "What the hell is going on with you two?"

Mary, "Tom, I need you to listen this time, this is important."

Tom sits back and lifts his hands in a motion of okay.

Mary, "Vickie was raped a few weeks ago. I just got back from the doctor and he confirmed it and she is pregnant."

Tom sits up and looks at both in disbelief. "Who did this?"

"Vickie says that Derek drugged her and raped her at his house."

"That's crap! Derek thinks the world of her. Vickie, who really did this? I bet it was some boyfriend you teased and he finally got you."

Vickie starts crying. "No, Daddy, it was not a boyfriend, it was Derek. He tried kissing me earlier that day and when I refused him he gave me a soda with drugs in it. I woke up and it was done to me."

Tom gets up and picks up the phone to call Derek. "Sherry, let me talk to Derek."

Derek comes on the line.

Tom, "Derek, did you touch my little girl a few weeks ago?"

Mary and Vickie only hear mumbles and can't make out what Derek is saying.

Tom, "Well, Vickie claims you kissed her and touched her."

Derek offers a long explanation as Tom's face turns red. In the middle of hearing it, Tom slams the phone, hanging up on Derek. He sits back down and looks at Vickie. "Bet you were acting like a little prostitute around Derek weren't you? Weren't you!"

Vickie replies, "No!"

Mary, "Tom, she did nothing wrong!"

Tom, "Shut up, Mary, you are just as big of a whore as she is."

Vickie, "He drugged me, Dad. I did not lead him on."

Tom looks at Mary. "You raised her to be one just like you, and now she is pregnant by her cousin."

Vickie is crying, holding onto her mom.

Mary, "Tom, please, it is not that way."

Tom gets up looking around and then walks off to the bedroom. Tom emerges with his pistol as Mary screams, "Tom, what are you doing with that gun?"

Tom, "I am going to kill him for screwing my slut daughter."

Mary, "Please don't go, please don't do this. You will just make things worse."

Tom ignores her leaving to his car and driving off. Mary runs to the phone and calls Derek's house.

Mary, "Sherry, you need to all leave, Tom is coming over to your house, and he has his gun."

Sherry, "Mary, what are you talking about? Derek is over here nervous, what is going on?"

Mary, "Derek drugged and raped Vickie and Tom has lost control. I think he intends to harm Derek."

Sherry, "Oh my God!" The phone hangs up as Sherry turns to Derek. "Derek, that was Mary, Tom is heading over here with a gun."

Derek jumps up and runs to his room and comes back with a shotgun.

"Derek, did you do something to Vickie."

"I did a horrible thing, I could not control myself."

Sherry slowly walks backward. "Oh, Derek!"

"I'm sorry, honey."

Suddenly at that moment, the door kicks in and it is Tom. Instinctively Derek turns around and fires his shotgun at Tom knocking him backward on to the lawn. Sherry screams as Derek walks slowly to the front door. He looks down at Tom and Tom whimpers, "My little girl. Victoria." Tom's head falls to one side and he dies.

Derek drops to his knees crying. "Tom, Tom!" Silence gives way to sirens as police arrive.

It is For the Better

THE POLICE ARRESTED Derek for the shooting but he was given probation for the homicide. No one told authorities what was the cause for Tom's rage so it was ruled as an alcoholic rage. Derek was cleared of the shooting but police had found illegal prescriptions in his home that often are used for date rape drugging. Derek had signed the home to Mary, and they had nothing to do with each other from then on. Tom's funeral was simple as there was nothing left for Mary and Vickie to live on. Mary worked at a nursing home to make ends meet, but they were tighter than when Tom was alive. Vickie has grown scared at the prospect of raising a child and especially one from her cousin. The only thing she can think of is the rape every time she sees her belly getting bigger. Mary has convinced her to give the baby up for adoption. Vickie feels like she has no choice because without her mom's support it would not be possible to raise this child.

She feels trapped and alone in the world. Her depression causes her to cut on herself and sometimes seems distant. She sees different people to help her but nothing seems to clear the fog of her mind. She just seems to go with whatever people tell her do. It is not hard for authorities to agree that the child needs to leave that environment when born.

Vickie's day comes to deliver the child and after its birth, she is only given a few seconds to see her little girl. Vickie cries as they take the little girl away as she has already been adopted before she was born. Vickie feels dead inside—lost and unworthy. She is told it was all for the better, but that does not beguile the feelings she feels about herself. Her only oasis is school work. She seems to excel even better than before. There is a focus that she uses to bury herself into her work. She was already on the honor roll but is doing better than most. Vickie has turned seventeen and has no plans for the future. She has become an empty shell, quiet and retracted. She is sent to a crises prevention psychologist because of fear that she would kill herself. It is believed this response from an apparent cry for help as she was cutting on her arms. She sits in a chair next to Dr. Smith just staring at the ground with shoulders slumped.

Smith, "Vickie, Vickie?"

Vickie looks toward his general direction. "What?"

"Vickie, we need to get you out your shell and talk about everything that has happened. Let's start with the cutting on your arms. Why do you feel the need to do that?"

Vickie looks at the scars on her arms, those healing from past wounds and those recent. "I don't know."

"You don't know why?"

Vickie turns her arm around. "No. However what fascinates me is that I don't feel pain when cutting them."

"You don't feel pain?"

"I mean I feel the pain but it does not hurt as much as you would think, it does not bother me. That is so odd."

"The reason you don't feel the pain as much is because the trauma of recent events have caused so much emotional pain, your mind has numb itself to the pain. That numbness transposes to physical pain too. You are aware of it but you can handle it. Physical pain and emotional pain are all in your brain and can be controlled the same way."

"You are saying that my mind is blocking something really painful."

"That is correct."

Vickie sits up a little. "Then it will wear off."

"That is correct. Your trauma pain will diminish as the strength of the memory diminishes, then will your mind release you to deal with it full force. Some people develop block memories as if the trauma never happened, others pain control."

"Then how do any of us know what we see, hear, or know is real if our brains can manipulate our perception like that?"

Smith smiles. "You are a very bright, young lady. It happens all the time. If you video tape your life at one point and not watch the video for years later, you will find your memory of it quite a bit different." It grows quiet for a few minutes while Smith observes Vickie's expressions to determine what she is feeling.

"I have dreams that bother me."

"Tell me about them."

"Last night, I dreamed that I was in a jail for killing someone."

"Who did you kill?"

"I don't know, but it was someone who was harming someone I cared about. They were hurting them and I had to stop them. But I was considered wrong in stopping them."

"How did that make you feel being blamed for helping them?"

"It made me upset that life judged me as guilty of doing what was right."

"You feel killing someone is justified if you are protecting others?"

"Wouldn't you?"

"This is not about me."

"Yes, but I really was not trying to kill them but just stop them. It was horrible, I was stuck in that jail for the rest of my life."

"Losing your freedom scares you?"

"Yes. Not being in control of my life. I…I don't want to live without being control."

"Do you feel that way because of the rape and losing your child?"

Vickie just stares at the wall.

"Vickie. Vickie. Okay, why don't we talk about something else?"

Vickie just stares away.

"I am told you want to be an astronomer."

Vickie turns. "Not anymore."

"Why not?"

"That serves me no purpose anymore."

"What was about it that you liked?"

Vickie turns to Smith. "Let me ask you a question?"

"Okay."

"Why did you become a psychologist?"

"I wanted to help people."

"Really? I think that people originally pursue occupations because they are looking for answers."

"Interesting…and what answers do you think I was looking for?"

Vickie stares for a bit as Dr. Smith sits with a smug look on his face.

"I think you wanted to know why you were so screwed up." Smith's face moves to concern as Vickie continues, "Am I hitting close to the target? Why would anyone learn psychology unless they wanted to know what is wrong with themselves?"

"Don't be so judgmental, some of us enjoy understanding our fellow man."

"Then it is about power for you."

"It is about helping people."

"I think that is what you tell yourself but not the motivation."

The room is quiet for a minute while they stare at each other.

Smith, "I think we have made some progress today. We will continue this tomorrow. I want you to think about how to talk about the recent past events."

Vickie responds, "I want you to think about what we talked about today. Let's see if the reason you became a psychologist is still an issue." Vickie stands up as Smith slowly stands up. Vickie looks at him and leaves to the lobby where her mom awaits.

That night Smith calls Mary to discuss the first meeting.

Mary, "Do you think you can help her, Doctor?"

Smith, "I think so. She is different in many ways than what I am used to. She has a need to dominate other people, so I am letting her analyze me and do what she feels is getting to me, in order to draw her out."

"Why does she cut on herself?"

"We addressed that. That is a stress disorder manifesting itself in a way superficially. It is a cry for help."

"She is not going to kill herself is she?"

"No, she just needs to let out something and it really hurts her. Mrs. Newsome, are you okay?"

"I don't know, it has all been so confusing and horrible. Sometimes I feel like Vickie has a better handle on some of this than I do. Strange as that sounds."

"Not at all. Young people tend to repair themselves much quicker than older people. We tend to make things much more complex as we get older. She is a strong girl. I look forward to our appointment tomorrow."

"Thank you, Doctor, we will be there tomorrow."

They hang up as Mary looks at Vickie staring at a chessboard. Mary thinks, *I wish I knew how to help you.*

The next day at Smith's office, Vickie has returned for her next session. They sit quietly for a few minutes when Vickie opens up, "Did you figure out why you got into mind medicine?"

Smith, "Afraid I am still working on that one. However, can we talk about the recent events?"

"Sure why not."

"Okay, what do you think about most often?"

Vickie looks around a bit and kicks her heel repeatedly on the floor.

"Perhaps your dad?"

"That alcoholic, I don't think so."

"He is your dad though."

"He is a drinker and an abuser, that is all. Because of him we were always poor and had to move to the charity of others."

"Alcohol is a wheel that controls all the other wheels in the family machine."

"It will not control the machine anymore."

"Yes, but that leaves a void which you need to fill with what do you suppose?"

"Hate, is that what you want me to say?"

"You are a bright young lady, more learned and gifted than most your age. Don't let your good intellect keep you from feeling what you need to express. Our emotions are the same no matter what age we are. You ever hear the phrase that impression without expression leads to depression?"

"I like to think that a train can't move unless it is under a lot of steam pressure." Smith sits up. "Fascinating, Vickie, and I suppose you are the train."

"I understand that I must be in control of my life."

"That is good, nothing wrong with it. But too much pressure can explode. Think of cutting on yourself as cracks in the engine. You need to let off some of that steam."

Vickie looks down. "Is that why you were humoring me about why you got into this profession?"

"Humoring you, what do you mean?"

"I tried to get to you and throw you off from analyzing me. Instead of stopping me, you used that to figure out more about me. I know what you are doing. I am not fooled."

"No you are not."

"You are a good man. I like you. To answer your question, I think about my baby the most."

"Yes, Vickie, that is very hard. I can help you."

"Help me to understand why I let it happen."

"You were in emotional shock and unable to reason what to do. Your mother was your refuge and always had been. She was there to protect you and you obeyed her will."

"Was she right in what she made me do?"

"I am not going to apply blame or justify anything. My job is to help you categorize it in your mind so you can deal with it properly. After that, you can determine what is right or wrong."

"No one will control me anymore."

"Don't mistake control for help."

"I have done that already."

"Alcohol controlled your dad, didn't it?"

Vickie stops motionless and slowly moves her head to the ground.

"I am sorry, Vickie."

"Must we talk about him?"

"Yes."

"He was a weak man. I will never be involved with a man that drinks."

Time runs out as Smith says, "Vickie, I think we are making real progress and extremely fast."

"You are just very good at what you do I guess."

"No, you are a very strong lady and smart. The answers are already figured out in you, I think. It is only the emotions we need to get straight."

Vickie goes to the door. "Thank you."

Smith smiles. "You are welcome."

Vickie smiles leaving but with concerned thoughts running in her head. She spends the night sorting out things in her head. Like a puzzle putting itself together in her head, is seeing the big picture.

The next day, Vickie arrives for another session with Dr. Smith.

Smith, "Vickie, I have a surprise for you."

Vickie, "What is it?"

Smith hands Vickie a book that is about psychology. Vickie receives it and briefly looks at the print date and few first pages as Smith smiles on.

"Thank you."

"Your welcome. How are you feeling today?"

"Actually I am feeling better. I have been thinking a lot about my dad."

"Oh, what have you decided?"

"I have decided that I will control my life. I will obtain those things in life, like money that will help me control things."

"I understand the motivation but you should know that money, position are not really control. It is an illusion of control as you will always be governed by people that have a stake in things, whether it is the government or investors. Someone always controls the game and lets you control the small parts. Understand."

"I understand it very well now. It is clear what I must do."

"What must you do?"

"I must be the one that controls the game."

"That is quite a feat. How do you plan to get there?"

"Understand what another understands, know what others know, have others believe what I tell them."

Smith looks astonished. "Wow, how old are you?"

"Age is not important, only the realization of what is out there."

"You are a bright young lady, do not burn yourself out."

"My dad was an alcoholic and an abuser but he loved me. I loved him but hated his life. My mom is a victim and loved me. I love her but despise her weakness. My cousin raped me but he helped me through a lot of years. I thought of him as a father I did not have, but his kind will never hurt me again. I have arrived in my understanding that life is hard. I will strengthen myself and I will control what I possibly can."

"That is an impressive statement."

"Well, I think I no longer need these sessions anymore."

"Really why would you think that?"

"Your present to me tells me that."

"Oh?"

"This book is what brought you in psychology, right? I mean you worked out your issues with the help of this book and then decided to go into this work to help others."

Smith raises an eyebrow. "How did you figure out this?"

"Am I right?"

"Of matter of fact it is. That book brought me out of a dark time. I thought it might do the same for you."

"It will, not by reading it but the fact you just shared your whole past with me. You helped me."

"Inadvertently, it seems."

"That was your strategy from the beginning, was it not? I just simply finished it for you."

Smith stands up. "Vickie, you are going to do great things. Remember it is okay to feel sad once in a while, it is an emotion like happiness. Let yourself feel, just try not to obsess on it. Anyway, I only had these three sessions I could do for you. May I have a few minutes with your mother?"

Vickie stands and shakes Smith's hand. "Of course and thank you."

"Keep in touch, for my sake."

Vickie smiles and opens the door to motion to her mom. Mary walks up as Vickie. "Dr. Smith would like to converse with you."

Mary smiles as Vickie goes to the lobby and Smith closes the door.

Mary, "Doctor, were you able to get her out her shell?"

Smith, "The shell that you speak of is not a shell of hiding but one of metamorphosis. She is changing into something, something that is rare. I think what we are witnessing is the rebirth of someone new. Someone that will make a huge effect on the world around her. I know it seems lofty, but I see things in her that is hard to explain."

"My Vickie?"

Smith smiles. "In my professional opinion, she will be okay. She is about to channel those stressful emotions in ways that is going to rocket her to places."

"Okay but should she have medication or something?"

"No, the best medicine for her is let her figure it out."

"Are you sure?"

"Quite."

"So we are done here?"

"Yes, we are done here. Let me know if you need anything."

Mary looks confused. "Okay, well thank you, Doctor." She walks to the door and keeps turning looking confused as she opens it. She approaches Vickie to leave as Smith looks at Vickie and nods his head yes. Vickie smiles and leaves with her mom.

Vickie seems to remain quiet and withdrawn as she understands what to do but internally she sorts away at the emotions. She is in school and one teacher takes an interest in the quiet Vickie. He is an eccentric teacher who also holds motivational classes on the side. Chip Sanders likes to storm chase, race motorcycles, and do most things that involve adrenaline.

Chip, "Vickie, can I see you after class?"

Vickie, "Yes, sir."

After class, Chip sits down in the chair in front of Vickie.

Chip, "I know about your dad and I am sorry. Have you been to counseling?"

"Yes, but I don't think the counselors like my answers. Except one man who seem to help."

"What answers did you provide them with?"

Vickie holds her head with one arm braced on the desk. "They asked how do I handle people that wrong me. I told them I make them pay in ways unknown to them."

Chip laughs. "Yes, that would do it. What about the one who helped?"

"He had been through some things I have."

"Well that helps in talking to people."

Vickie smiles.

"Look, I am a motivational speaker, not a therapist but I have a few insights I could share if you like."

"Whatever."

"What killed the dinosaurs?"

Vickie sighs. "A meteor."

"Nope, it was cold and darkness later. You see they did not die immediately, they still had a life for a short while. It may have sucked but they were still alive for a while."

"And the point?"

"Just because the meteor lands on your world does not mean the end. You are alive so live it, understand?"

"I think so. You are telling me accept what has happened and live for today."

"That is right. Nothing is over yet. What do you want to be?"

"I want to be an astro—I mean, I am not sure anymore."

"You could be an astronomer, isn't that what you were about to say?"

"Not anymore."

"Why not?"

"That job has no power over people."

"Why do you need power over people?"

"So I can control what happens to me."

"That kind of control is an illusion. Be careful about putting walls up, you can barricade yourself so much, you miss the world around you."

"I have heard that before. I am not interested in the world. I just want to control people and never be poor."

"Well, sounds like you want to be an executive of a company."

Vickie looks up. "Yes, that is exactly what I want to do."

"Well, you have the brains for it. I will help you get there."

"I don't need help."

"We all need help. You can't get anywhere in this world without someone helping you. Also you can't get anywhere well without helping others."

Vickie looks at him. "I wished I could."

"You can and you must. If you don't help others, you can never be helped. It is just the way things work."

"I think I understand. It is just so hard."

"Life is hard, on everyone."

"Why do some people seem to have it so easy?"

"Everyone has problems, some just carry it better than others. Life is 90 percent how you react to it. You get back what you give. It is about living after the meteors hit."

Vickie gets up and starts to leave. "Thank you, Mr. Sanders."

Chip smiles as she leaves.

As the year progresses, Vickie maintains the honor roll and has maintained a weighted grade point average of 4.7, the highest in her entire school district. Scholarship offers have come from a handful of colleges already. Vickie has set her eyes on one college that several people in corporate power have earned from as well as politicians. She is following their path. Her vision to be in the corporate world is on track as she turned eighteen. Her mom seems to slow down and seems worn out. Vickie cares for her and starts to be focused on her needs. Mary has seemingly aged beyond her years. The toll of stress has been wearing her down. One evening, her mom says to her, "Vickie, you can do anything you want in your life."

"I know, Mom."

"I really wanted you to be an astronomer."

"I know, Mom, but I can't do that anymore. I need to go the direction I am headed."

"Vickie, I am sorry. I should have had you keep your child and we raised it together. I wish that I could see my granddaughter."

Vickie cries. "Mom, she is better off like you said."

"No, Victoria, a child needs their mother. I really did not know that well till now."

Vickie stands and looks out the window. "You have not called me that in years. Mom, I will be the most successful person you will ever see. I will climb the corporate ladder and make a name for myself. Nothing and no one will hold me back." Vickie turns around. "I will make you proud of me. Mom…Mom?" Vickie walks over as her mom is staring motionless. Vickie checks for pulse, breathing, and heart but nothing. She immediately calls 9-1-1 as she knows she is gone. Vickie sits next to her holding her mom's hand crying. "Mommy." Paramedics arrive to find that Mary had died of a heart attack. Again, Vickie faces another funeral and alone. Vickie is distant but focused; the tragedies of life seem to impact but no longer have the sting as before. She has become hard, hard like a rock.

She has inherited her home and her mom managed to carve out an insurance policy for enough money for Vickie to live on and go to college. She plans out her career path with the help of Chip. Vickie, as valedictorian, is to give a speech at her graduation. As her name is called the students roar as many know of her plight and victory over seemingly overwhelming odds. She smiles as she approaches the podium and teachers stand and clap. As the applaud dies down it becomes very quiet. Vickie stares out among the hundreds of students and parents. Even many other people hearing about Vickie have come to witness the person they have all heard about in their small town. Vickie looks at the podium with no speech written down, she begins to speak. "Thank you, everyone, for the warm applause. For years, I have lived in turmoil hoping for better days. As some of you know, I have been through the loss of my parents and many other things. I have not come here to tell you how I survived those times and managed to be on the honor roll. I could thank a number of people and even God and I do. Instead, I would like to say that where ever this life takes me I am thankful for every opportunity. I will take every hardship and fashion it into a shield to weather the next one. I will use every experience and make it a tool to deal with all other experiences. I will approach everyone as a friend until they prove themselves an enemy. I will stop those that mean to harm those I care about and move anyone or anything out my way. This I give to you as my mission, my oath, and my absolute promise." The students erupt in cheers as everyone stands and claps. Vickie smiles and looks down at the podium with concern. She takes a deep breath and smiles to everyone waving and leaving to her seat. The graduation ceremonies continue with all emotion to their end as it is noticeable that Vickie is gone. She has left to her home.

The weeks pass into solitude as everyone she has known from school has gone to enjoy their summer and prepare for their futures. For Vickie, it is only the preparation for the next phase of her calculated journey. Vickie prepares to leave as she has sold her old house and finishes packing and storing the last of her and her parent's possessions she has decided to keep; it all fits in her car easily. Chip helps her as he asks, "You going to miss the old home?"

Vickie looks around. "No, not really. Nothing but horrible memories here. I am going to start new. A new place, a new life, a new beginning."

Chip smiles. "I am proud of you, Vickie."

"I would not have made it if it was not for you and others too."

"I have a feeling you would have landed on your feet anyway. It might have taken a bit longer but you are a survivor."

Vickie smiles. "Well, I guess this is it."

"One last thought before you go?"

"I would love it."

"You have been through the heat, extreme heat. That heat just tempers you stronger. That strength people will need. Don't shy away from it. It is a fire that lives within in you and will consume you unless you use it correctly. Don't let it burn you up, let it fuel you with purpose."

"You may make a successful motivational speaker yet."

"I only need to motivate one person to be successful."

Chip hugs Vickie. "Take care of yourself."

"Thank you for everything."

Chip motions to wait as he reaches in his car. He returns with a stemmed rose. Vickie looks at it and says, "It is beautiful."

Chip, "It is you."

Vickie smiles and gets in the old car of her parents. She drives off as Chip watches.

The Real Education Starts

FIRST DAY OFF to college is a bright sunny day as Vickie feels like a new person with a sense of freedom. At the same time, she is a little nervous but she soon acclimates to the environment. As she drags her luggage to the dorm room, a group of guys stare at her.

One guy says, "More meat for my grinder."

His friend slaps him in the chest. "Hey knock it off."

Vickie looks at the friend named John Patterson and smiles. John looks like a deer in headlights as he stares back. Time seems to slow down as he stares at the tall statuesque Vickie with blond long hair and piercing light blue eyes. John's friend looks at both and waves his hand in front of John's face. Vickie just leaves into the dorm building which breaks the spell John is under. He notices his friends are already leaving as he looks back at the dorm a couple of times then catches up to his friends. She reaches the dorm room and meets her roommate, Cindy Jones. The room is a single room with a bathroom and shower attached. Each side of the room has small beds with shelves on the wall next to them. On the opposite side of the room from the door is a window and long shelf. Cindy has already placed some minor appliances, microwave on it.

Cindy, "Are you my new roomy?"

Vickie, "Appears so. Vickie is my name, Vickie Newsome."

"Cindy Jones, nice to meet you."

They shake hands as she helps Vickie put things away. Cindy notices Vickie is very quiet person. "So where are you from?"

"Hemdale, you know where that is?"

"Oh yea. Passed through there once."

"Really? I am surprised, not a terribly big place."

"Well, my parents and I were exploring college campuses last year and some guy at a gas station told us to go through Hemdale to come here. Turns out the old man took us the long way around."

Vickie stops and asks, "Did he have blue coveralls, dark hair?"

"Yea, that is exactly what he looks like. You've seen him?"

"I remember a man who gave us directions at an old gas station. He had a dog that sat next to a rocking chair at the front of his porch."

"That is him. What a coincidence."

"Yea, that is weird."

"Anyway, I am from Columbus. It was hard moving from home, was it hard for you?"

"No, not really, my parents died and I simply sold everything and came here."

"I am so sorry."

"Don't worry, I am good, starting new."

"I am so glad you are here, I hear horror stories about bad roommates. My older sister already graduated college, and she had a roommate that partied and was drunk half the time."

"I don't like alcohol. I just want to get on with this so I can move on to a career."

"I like to drink but not drunk. I hope you have a little fun happen."

"Not sure what fun is."

Cindy walks over to Vickie and puts her arm around her. "I will show you."

Vickie smiles. "Okay."

They finish putting clothes away.

Cindy sits on her bed. "What are you going for?"

"Degree? I want a business degree."

"Oh, math, finance ewww. I want to be a psychologist."

"I seem to be scheduled for math, political science, economics, English, and physical education."

"I got some of the same subjects. I guess they start us all in the basics no matter what our degree will be. What are you taking for PE?"

"Is there a self-defense here?"

"Sure is but I am taking bowling."

"Bowling?"

"Yes bowling."

Vickie smiles. "Okay."

Vickie leaves to sign up for PE and sees the teacher of Shotokan karate and Aikido Sensei Sato Takashi as she hands her signup sheet to him.

Sato, "Domo."

Vickie, "Excuse me?"

"It is a basic thank you in Japanese."

"Oh, Domo."

Sato smiles. "What are you interested in taking?"

"I was interested in self-defense."

"You want to learn to protect yourself, that is important especially on a college campus."

"Really, is there a huge problem?"

"There is campus police but they can't be everywhere all the time. You have fifteen thousand students at this university full of hormone, alcohol charged, "just out of high school only adults in the legal age" definition. What do you think?"

"Sounds like I need to learn self-defense. What about more than just self-defense?"

"We teach two styles here: karate and Aikido."

"What's the difference?"

"Karate is what most people are familiar with. It means *empty hands* which is no weapons. It is more the punching, kicking stuff you may have seen on TV. Then there is Aikido which is based on sword movement but without the swords. It is a reactive martial arts, more of what we base our basic self-defense course off of."

"How long does it take to learn these?"

"How long will you live?"

Vickie gives a confused look.

Sato laughs. "There is no end to learning it. Your body changes over time, you mind changes so the learning is adaptive. But to be proficient in karate depends on how much effort you put in, maybe two and half years if you work hard. Aikido you are looking at five years."

"What about belts, black belt, red belt, so on."

"We have belts in karate but not in Aikido. Belts represent ranks and those ranks are in Aikido just like karate. Belts were introduced in karate originally to help visually help motivate students. Originally there was just the ranks. White belt through brown are called *Kyu* which is your beginning grades or rank. It basically means young or boy. When you reach black belt that is the ranks called *Dan* which means masterful or man."

"I want to be a Dan in both."

"Ambitious, are you here for four years or more?"

"Don't you have a school outside the campus?"

Sato smiles. "Yes, I have a dojo which is where my most serious students are."

"How much would it cost to learn after PE as well?"

"It is affordable but let's see you take it here on campus first and see if you want to go further. Besides, I don't take in everyone."

"Money means nothing to you, is that a Zen thing?"

"Money is not the issue. It is a great responsibility teaching things I know. Especially to someone that has no moral restraint in hurting people."

"I don't plan to hurt people."

"If you are taking martial arts, you are planning to hurt someone, even in self-defense. It is what manner will you understand this. A great karate master was walking down the road and was robbed at knife point. He struck the robber with a two-fist strike crippling the robber. He felt bad about it and realized it was not worth the money and bread he was carrying. Result, now he gave the robber purpose in trying revenge. The martial arts is about having power but being confident not just in your ability to defend yourself but when not to. As far as Zen, that is not what you think."

"I think I understand."

"Do you?"

"I will be back for my first lesson."

Vickie walks a bit and turns around. "Oh and by the way, I will let Zen do its own thinking."

Sato smiles. "When you come back you will be coming for your second lesson."

Vickie leaves back to her dorm to prepare for her schedule and to read her syllabus.

Vickie arrives for her math class and Cindy sits next to her.

Cindy, "I hate math."

Vickie, "I love it. It is predictable, in order. It does what it is supposed to do."

"Geek."

Vickie smiles and pans around the room looking at the other students until her eye catches one guy staring at her. She recognizes him from the group of boys earlier that defended her. He smiles at Vickie as Vickie gives a half smile back.

Vickie, "Cindy, who is that boy behind my left shoulder two rows up that is staring at me?"

Cindy, "I don't know but I have seen him before, I think. Oh my God are you already trolling for a guy?"

"No, he just mentioned something when I first came on campus."

Vickie looks back as John has moved to the row behind her.

Vickie, "Are you going to sit behind me all the time?"

John, "Sorry, I was hoping to introduce myself."

"Well you are here."

"John Patterson."

"Vickie."

They shake hands as John asks, "Just Vickie."

"Good enough."

"Okay, that is okay."

"Good. And thank you for defending me earlier."

"No problem."

Class finishes and Vickie and Cindy leave as John runs up to them.

John, "Hey after the next couple of classes would you like to hang out?"

Cindy, "Vickie, I got to go to my next class, see you later?"

Vickie, "See you later, Cindy." Vickie turns to John. "Look, John, I am not looking for a boyfriend. I am just here to learn."

"So am I but it would be nice to have a companion in this learning thing."

"Learning thing? Get to your next class."

Vickie smiles and walks off as John stares at her leaving. John thinks, *I like her.*

The Master

T HE WEEKS PROGRESS and Vickie is excelling in her courses. She is in her dorm room as Cindy was pulling her hair. "Ahhhh, I hate math!"

Vickie sits by her. "Look, it is just a matter of framing your mind to understanding the concepts. It is no different than learning English. You simply change the frame template for each subject. Everything in math is about patterns, if you see the patterns, it makes sense."

Cindy looks at her book. "I don't see a pattern."

"These numbers here will always show in pairs like this. So whenever you see them, they will come again here, you see?"

Cindy stares for a bit. "Yea, I think I see it. So if those two do that then it means the variable works like this?"

"Exactly, see not that hard. The patterns never change, only the complexity of the formulas."

Cindy smiles. "Are you sure you don't want to be in psychology?"

"Ah, no. Well, I am off to my martial arts class."

"How is that going by the way."

"It is physically demanding, like boot camp. You have to get in shape before they give you advanced techniques."

"Better you than me."

"It also relieves stress from all this book work. Why don't you join me?"

"Sorry I will stick to golf."

"I thought it was bowling?"

"I changed it today."

Vickie laughs. "Okay, see you after a while."

Vickie arrives at the dojo of Sensei Sato for her lessons of the evening. She begins her exercise patterns that help her learn muscular memory for the techniques she will learn later. Sato has two other instructors that help and he watches Vickie practice. Through the evening, the students line up for dismissal. Sato calls Vickie out and hands her a yellow belt for karate. Everyone claps as she puts on her new belt rank.

Sato, "Vickie, let's talk when you get changed."

Vickie bows and leaves to the changing room. As she returns, she sits next to Sato who is staring at a book. Vickie patiently waits for her sensei to speak.

Sato, "Do you know decades ago the martial arts were illegal in Japan? So students would in secret train from their teachers."

Vickie, "That is hard to imagine since it seems Japan is so associated with karate."

"Long before that there was a school that only took several students in a year. Once you were in, you lived and worked there. This student was not allowed to train with the others for a very long time. He even attacked his master which the master easily defeated him and put him back to work. Later, he was called in and shown a circle painted on a paper. The master told the student that 'If you understand this, you will know everything you need to know about the martial arts.' He then dismissed him from the school. The student became one of the greatest swordsman of all time. He even wrote a book of strategy that it is even used in business today." Sato closes the book and hands it to Vickie.

"Is this that book?"

"Yes."

"Thank you, Sensei Takashi, I mean *domo*."

Sato smiles. "Vickie, I have seen one other person like you in life. You are not studying the martial arts for leisure or physical fitness, you are training with a purpose in mind. You are preparing for something that you know you should. Know that the martial arts is not all about beating an opponent up, it is about life and strategy. No one picks a fight with a tiger. Starting tomorrow after class if you can manage it, I will start training you in Aikido as well as karate. It will be hard, but you will need it."

Vickie with an astonished look on her face. "I am honored, I will work very hard."

Sato slaps her on the knee and stands up to bow as she stands and bows. Vickie walks back to her campus as it is very dark. She sees two men down the street as she walks toward them. They turn and notice this pretty young girl walking toward them.

As she approaches, one of the men say, "Hey beautiful, would you like a date tonight?"

She stops and looks at him.

The other man says, "I have some party favors." He holds his hand out with some pills in it. They both laugh and the laughs stop as one of the men stare at an intense stare from Vickie. Eventually they start to back up and move to the side as Vickie walks slowly by them staring and then leaves. Out of the shadows, Sato steps out and says in a soft mumble to himself, "Tiger."

Summer of Fun

S UMMER APPROACHES AS classes end. In the dorm room, Cindy packs to go back to her parent's house for the summer.

Cindy, "Vickie, what are you going to do for the summer, you never told me."

Vickie, "I have martial classes I am committed to and want to keep studying."

"Boring! Why don't you come over to my parents for a while. We will go have some fun."

"Thank you, no."

"Your loss but if you change your mind, call me. You are always welcome."

"Thank you, Cindy, tell your parents hi."

Cindy heads to the door. "Vickie, please have some fun."

Vickie smiles. "I am having fun, trust me. This is the best I have had it in my whole life."

Cindy gives a concerned look and then smiles to leave. Vickie is reading a novel as a knock on the door interrupts. "Yes."

John walks in. "Hi, Vickie, can I come in?"

Vickie, "So were you just waiting for my roommate to leave?"

John walks in. "I might have. Hey we have an end-of-the-season party tonight at my frat house."

"I don't think so."

"One party and I will leave you alone for the summer."

"You probably are leaving for the summer anyway."

"Yea, but the offer is still the same."

"I have a book to read."

"Really? C'mon, you can leave whenever you want."

Vickie laughs. "I know I can. All right, I will meet you there."

"You know where it is?"

"Of course, everyone knows about that place."

"You see, our reputation precedes us."

"All right get out here before I change my mind."

John laughs; "All right, all right, I am gone. Don't let me down. Got to have the prettiest girl by my side."

"Leave!"

John leaves laughing as Vickie shakes her head smiling.

John is at the frat party drinking a plastic cup of beer when one of his friends says, "Where is this girlfriend of yours?"

John, "She will be here."

John's friend, "Give it up, pal, there are a million girls here."

"Not like this one."

His friend replies, "Whatever, pal."

At that moment, John's friends look at the front door as Vickie walks in with a red dress on and makeup. One of the guys says, "Holy smokes!"

John tells his friends, "Now, that is what I am waiting for."

Vickie walks up to John as his friends stare in disbelief at the beauty they are witnessing. They have seen her before but in regular clothes and not dolled up. She looks like she stepped off the cover of a magazine.

John to his friends, "Put your tongues back in, guys."

Vickie, "John, is this acceptable?"

John, "You have no idea. Get you a beer."

"No, thank you, I am fine."

John says, "Don't you guys have a million other girls to attend to?"

His friends walk off shaking their head.

John, "Sorry, Vickie, they have just never seen you like this before."

Vickie, "And you have?"

John takes a drink. "No."

"This is a nice place."

"Nice and expensive, but it is the place to be for a guy. Why did you get so dressed up? Was it for me?"

"Yes, I wanted you to be proud. Did it work?"

"Oh yes."

"I have to make a confession. I have been watching you all year."

"I know you are, and you have tried so hard to make an impression on me. The reality is you have. I just have things I am trying to accomplish and the last thing I need is a boyfriend."

"I am sorry you don't have time for a boyfriend. You are a very interesting person and look how toned you are. Those martial classes have done you good."

"Thank you, John, you are a good guy."

"Look, I know I am a dime a dozen guy going through college so I know there is nothing I am that can attract someone like you."

"I think you have me too much on a pedestal, John. I am nobody special myself. I am just not here to get my MRS degree like some girls."

John looks puzzled. "MRS, what is that?"

"MRS as in Mrs. Married, looking for a professional man to marry."

"Yea, I know what you mean, I know a couple of girls like that. I guess they have to go to college to find a guy like us. Why don't they focus on an actual career?"

"Because their goal is marriage, kids, but they have to fish in the right pond to catch the right fish. That is not me."

They look around while Vickie asks, "John, you don't seem to fit this fraternity."

"Yea, the guys here think of me as kind of boring but the beer is good."

"Be careful of that stuff, it can make you into someone you don't want to be."

"No problem, I control it, not it me."

Vickie gives a smirk. "Right."

They walk over as John fills up his cup of beer.

John, "I really am in control of it, just my second cup. Let's dance."

Vickie, "Okay, but I am not much of a dancer."

"Me neither, just imagine we are at the prom."

"Never went to the prom."

"I don't believe that no one asked you."

"They did but I was just not in a place to socialize like that."

They begin to dance; as the evening carries on John begins to show signs of getting tired.

John, "Hey, can we stop now?"

Vickie and John leave to a quieter part of the house.

John, "You are not even breaking a sweat."

Vickie, "It is all that training."

"You really like that martial stuff."

"It is more than like, it is a need. Look, I had a great time, but I want to go."

"Oh, well let me walk you home."

"No, that is ok, you just enjoy yourself." Vickie kisses John on the cheek and smiles.

John smiles. "Good night, Vickie, thank you for coming."

Vickie turns as she walks away and gives a smile. John's friends slap him on the shoulder and say, "If you don't tap that, I will kick your butt myself."

John laughs. "Where's the beer."

They go and John drinks himself to a drunken state.

Vickie arrives at the dorm room and stares at the bathroom mirror with a smile on her face. Her smile disappears as the past washes over her. She begins to hastily undress and shower the beauty off her. She prepares for bed and begins to read her book again. After a few minutes, she puts the book down and walks over to the bathroom floor to pick up the red dress. She puts it on a hanger and puts it up on the bathroom door to back away and look at it. She smiles and lays down to stare at the ceiling pondering the evening that has passed.

The dorm is quiet and mostly empty as Vickie wakes up and gets dressed for the day. She opens her dorm room door and finds John passed out on the floor. She rolls him over and slaps him awake. He comes to groggy and disoriented.

Vickie, "Lord, unbelievable." She drags him in the dorm room out view of anyone that might still be there. She makes a cup of coffee and tells John to drink. He complains about a severe headache. Vickie, "You are dehydrated, that is what alcohol does. You should have drank water last night."

John, "I'm sorry, Vickie, but you left and I just had a few more drinks."

"I am sure it was more than a few. How did you even make it here?"

"I wanted to say good night."

"Keep drinking the coffee."

After a while, John begins to become coherent as Vickie puts her book down.

Vickie, "You a person again?"

John, "Holy hell, that was a bad one."

He looks up at Vickie. "I am so sorry, Vickie."

"It is okay, John. It is a party."

"No, I am sorry, that was inexcusable."

"As soon as you feel better, you may go."

John gets up. "I will go now."

"I did not say right now."

"I have embarrassed myself enough. I will see you later, Vickie."

"Take care, John."

John shakes his head yes and leaves. Vickie combs her hair through fingers and exhales.

Sophomore and More

VICKIE HAS MANAGED to avoid John for most of the summer, ever increasing her martial arts training. Cindy comes back for fall season and sees Vickie is more toned and stronger looking. The two embrace happy to see each other.

Cindy, "Oh my God, look at you! You are so hard looking."

Vickie, "Sexy, huh?"

"I am not a lesbian but you are tempting me."

"Stop it. How was your summer?"

"Boring with my parents but I went on a couple of trips. You should have been with me."

"There were a few times I wished I had."

"What happened?"

"John is what happened. Beginning of the summer I found him passed out drunk at our dorm door. He stayed away for a couple of weeks but then someone got me and asked me to come get him. Like I am his keeper. I guess they thought we are a couple. Anyway, he was drunk and passed out on someone's lawn and a couple of campus girls saw him and recognized him. I avoided him for a month but he came back all nice and apologetic. Then showed up at the burger joint down the street drunk and trying to talk to me. I brought him here and cleaned him up. When he sobered had a long talk with him. He seemed to straighten up after that but I think he has a drinking problem."

"Oh wow, what are you going to do?"

"I am not sure. He seems to be turning into my cross to bear. I just can't stand the drinking though, it pisses me off. It is what my dad used to do all the time. Sometimes I could just beat the crap out of John."

"Sounds like someone likes John."

"I like him but not when he drinks."

"Maybe you like him because he is like your dad."

"I know the dad complex thing. I get at what you are saying. He is a good guy and cute, he just needs to stay sober."

"Look, I fully intend to delve into your love life deeper but for now I need to go and take care of some school stuff."

"All right, go, and forget about that there is a love life because there is not. Don't have time for it."

Cindy gets up to leave. "Right."

Vickie smiles as she continues reading the book she was working on.

Vickie finishes up her martial arts class and walks back to her dorm when she sees John waiting in her path.

She thinks, *Here we go.*

John starts to walk beside her quietly. After a few moments, he says, "I stopped drinking."

Vickie looks up. "Really?"

John, "Yes, I am done with that."

"Why?"

"Why? Because if I don't you won't have anything to do with me and I like you."

"I like you too John but that is no reason to quit. At least it is a reason that will not last."

"Anything that takes me away from you is not going to be in my life."

"And when I am no longer in your life, what then? You see, John, you have to quit for yourself."

"I want to, I mean I am. I don't want it anymore."

"I think you are a borderline alcoholic."

"Have I ever hit you?"

"That just means you are not a mean drunk. Besides if you tried, I would lay you out all over this ground."

John jeers. "You are probably right. You have really grown tough looking but still hot as ever."

Vickie smiles.

John, "Look, please give me another chance."

They are quiet for a while and Vickie responds, "You have given up drinking for good?"

John nods his head yes.

"All right, good. By the way, you don't mind if I date your friend Kevin do you?"

"Kevin, Kevin Lesterson?"

"Yes."

"Well, he will be happy to know that but what about us?"

"I was just using you to get to Kevin."

John looks away in disgust. "You are joking with me, right?"

"Sorry, no."

John stares at Vickie as she looks back and then they stop walking.

John, "Well…okay. Okay."

Vickie, "Are you all right, John?"

"Fine, I am just fine. Look, I need to go."

John walks quickly away toward his frat house as Vickie looks down and then back up at him. She continues on to her dorm.

Cindy is filling out papers as Vickie walks in quietly.

Cindy, "What's wrong?"

Vickie, "John told me he has stopped drinking."

"Well, that is good, right?"

Vickie is staring at the ground.

Cindy, "Right?"

Vickie looks up and smiles. "I don't think he understands how alcohol really works so I broke up with him. Told him I wanted to be with his friend Kevin."

"Why?"

"I am testing John."

"You shouldn't play with people like that, it could backfire on you."

"There is nothing to backfire. I can afford to lose John."

"Well that is so awesome of you, Vickie. You have the ability to throw people away so easily. How do I get that superpower?"

"Not a power, just self-protection."

"Self-protection, more like not wanting anyone to like you too much."

Vickie looks at Cindy with a stern stare.

"Look I'm sorry. I just think you need to ease up a bit on John."

"Maybe, but he needs to stop drinking. You just don't know how bad that kind of thing can get."

Vickie stands up and stares at a picture of her mom saying quietly, "You just don't know."

Cindy looks at Vickie with sadness. Vickie turns and sees Cindy and smiles. As Vickie sits down on the bed, Cindy asks, "What keeps you going?"

Vickie, "I am not sure, I really don't. It is like I was put in a slingshot and the momentum is a force that I can't stop."

"What happens when all that pain and anger loses fuel?"

Vickie stares for a moment. "It would mean my purpose is finished."

Cindy looks puzzled. "That is not purpose, just mania."

"Maybe, but it serves my purpose."

"You genuinely scare me, Vickie."

"You have nothing to worry about unless you get in my way."

Cindy has a concerned look as Vickie smiles.

"Just kidding…maybe."

Vickie gets up and laughs. Cindy watches her leave and shakes her head in disbelief.

As the day passes into evening, Vickie goes to her martial arts classes. It is dark and the school is lit up where people passing by can watch the students train. Cindy stands at a safe distance to keep Vickie from seeing her. Vickie is wearing a brown belt and as she practices various karate moves. The room divides as the students sit along the wall. Vickie stands in the center as another student, who is a black belt, squares off with her. The instructor gives the signal to start and they spar. The movement is almost dizzying as Vickie kicks the black belt student into other students sitting. The instructor calls stop as Cindy has a disturbed look on her face. The instructor calls another student black belt who has two stripes on his black belt, meaning second-degree black belt. He calls start and the two slowly move around each other. This student is much better than the last, and Vickie barely manages to avoid getting hit. The student throws punches and kicks in combination that are perfect and timed like a ballet. Vickie watches the student as he makes another assault and is staggering backward as

Vickie has landed a punch into his sternum. He composes himself to make another run. He does the same technique but this time manages to hit Vickie as she spins around and drops him with a kick to his hip. The instructor calls stop. Cindy is further stunned and becomes scared that in just over a year Vickie is already beating black belts. Cindy begins to leave looking back once in a while walking slowly but makes her way back to the dorm. Vickie stands as the instructor tells her, "You will now compete against me."

Vickie nods her head yes as Sensei Sato who has been standing watching stops his instructor, "Wait!" Sato walks up and relieves his instructor, "You will fight me in this contest."

Vickie looks around at the other students as this is a very rare occurrence to see the master spar. They square off and bow as Vickie watches carefully her sensei's moves. He moves calmly and slowly staring at her hips to judge her capable movements. She throws a couple of combinations which he seems to just brush away and stand next to her as if they were dancing. She backs away quickly realizing she is out her league.

Sato says, "Like a fruit that waits for the perfect moment to fall from the tree, you must move then." She takes a deep breath, exhales, and slowly moves toward him and then throws a punch that he quickly blocks and moves out the way. He holds his hand up to stop. They both bow as he smiles and walks away.

Later that night Vickie walks into the dorm room as Cindy is laying in bed. Vickie is holding a black belt. Cindy says, "Congratulations."

Vickie, "Thank you, I was not expecting this so soon. It usually takes two years or more to reach first Dan in karate."

"Yea, well most people just go a day a week to karate class, not almost every night, plus PE time at college and practice in their own time."

"I know you think I am obsessed about this but no man will ever make me a victim."

"Man?"

"Yes man because that is what I have to worry about."

"When is it going to be enough, when you reach twenty-degree black belt?"

"Funny. There is only ten degrees and the last few are more honorable and about position than skill."

"Whatever, how much karate does one need?"

"I am also in Aikido too. I plan to take several other things too."

"I simply don't understand it but as long as you don't use it on me."

Vickie smiles. "Take it easy, Cin."

How Dry I Am

Vickie shows up one evening at John's frat house to go out with Kevin. Kevin shows up and ask her, "You ready, Vick?"

Vickie, "Oh yes."

John is walking in and stops to see them leaving.

Kevin, "Don't stay up, John."

Vickie looks at John as he looks jealous and a bit sad. They continue on as John stares. Kevin drives Vickie to a drive-in movie.

Vickie says, "I have not seen one of these in ages."

Kevin, "Yea, they are rare these days but can be fun. It is not too cold?"

"No, it is just right."

"When did you go to a drive-in?"

"It was after we moved to Hemdale to stay with my uncle. He took us all one night and it was awesome."

As they watch the movie, it is obvious that Vickie's mind is not on the movie. Kevin asks, "Can I ask you something?"

Vickie turns. "Sure."

Kevin, "You like John, don't you?"

"He is a cool guy."

"And now?"

"My dad was an alcoholic and John drinks too much."

Kevin looks around and says, "You have no idea how great it is going out with you. You are gorgeous and strong looking. You certainly have the attention of just about everyone. But John is my friend and I have to be honest. He is stuck on you."

"I know he likes me."

Kevin laughs. "More than like, that boy is in love."

"He confessed that to me."

"Did not have to, he has not had a drink in months."

"Really?"

Kevin nods yes. "I get the feeling you like him too."

Vickie looks down. "I am sorry, Kevin, you feel that way."

"It is all right, I got to hang out with a hot babe."

Vickie smiles and snuggles next to him to watch the movie. Kevin smiles as well and watches the movie as well. After the movie and Kevin is driving back to his frat house to park. "I will walk you back to your dorm."

Vickie, "No, that is okay, I like to be alone now."

Vickie begins to walk away as Kevin says, "Vickie, thank you for a good time. I hope things work out between you and John."

Vickie walks up to Kevin and kisses him on the cheek, smiles, and walks away. As Vickie approaches her dorm, she hears. "Vickie."

John emerges and walks up to her.

Vickie, "You waited for me?"

John, "I did a lot of walking and thinking."

"What did you figure out?"

"What I have lost." John stares at the ground, kicking the dirt.

Vickie walks up to John and holds his chin up. "You have not lost anything. Kevin told me that you have not had a drink in months. I never stopped liking you, I just needed you to stop drinking."

"What about Kevin?"

"He was just a date once in a while. I never stop thinking about you."

"Really?"

"Really. Tomorrow night is my first night at the martial arts class in helping instructing students. Come watch me?"

John has a huge grin. "I would love to."

Vickie kisses him on the lips as they both stare at each other. John kisses her back as it seems to last forever. They both break apart almost in a daze.

Vickie, "Ummm, see you at class tomorrow?"

John, "Sure."

Vickie grabs his finger and holds it smiling. "Good night, Johnny."

"Night."

Vickie walks to her dorm looking back once in a while as John stares. He watches her leave and walks back to his frat house with a sense of happiness that washes over him like a warm tide. As John arrives in his room, Kevin is watching TV.

John says, "Kev."

Kevin looks up. "What's up, John?"

"Thanks."

Kevin looks away a bit and realizes what he is talking about. "Oh, you're welcome."

It's All About Cindy

JOHN CATCHES UP with Vickie and they go to her night karate class. He sits down in a row of chairs set aside for spectators. The students and instructors walked out dressed for the evening of training. Vickie is called out by Sensei Sato to lead the students in exercises. John watches attentively even though it seems somewhat boring to him. Vickie looks over once in a while and smiles at him. He just smiles back as he pans around the room. It has pictures of past martial arts heroes, famous for their contributions in the arts. He sees flags and decorations with Japanese writing as he ponders what it all means. Vickie handles a small group of students showing them techniques as the other instructor works with the more advanced students. After class, everyone starts to leave and Vickie comes out changing clothes. John walks up as Sato meets them.

Vickie, "Sensei, this is my boyfriend John."

John looks at Vickie as she stares indirectly at John and back to Sato.

Sato extends his hand out. "Nice to meet you, John."

John, "Nice to meet you, sir."

Sato, "Sato, please just call me Sato. It is good to meet a close friend of Vickie."

"Well, I have passed by here a few times but it is different seeing it from inside."

"Does our classes interest you?"

"Oh no, I am no good at this stuff. I will just stick with football and stuff."

"Well, the concepts here work for anything. It is good to meet you, John. Vickie, see you tomorrow."

Vickie bows as Sato leaves. Vickie grabs John's arm and slings her duffle bag around her shoulder. As they leave, John says, "You are really good."

Vickie, "Thank you, John, it was a pretty easy evening. Usually, I am training with several advanced students and sometimes Sato himself."

"He looks like a badass."

"I could only hope to be half as good as him. He has an understanding of human psychology that would shame most professors. He has ways of tricking your mind and fools your instinct."

"Well, I won't be messing with him."

"Ah no."

John and Vickie arrive at her dorm room and walk in laughing at some joke John told. But laughter stops suddenly as Cindy is crying holding her face.

Vickie, "Cindy, what is wrong?"

Cindy looks up and her face is bruised and has a black eye.

Vickie, "Oh my God, what happened?"

"I was walking from the store and two guys asked me if I wanted to party." Cindy cries some. "I told them no and they grabbed me." Cindy cries as John kneels down next to her and Vickie.

Vickie, "Tell me what did they do?"

"They tried to make me swallow some pill but I spit it out in the tall one's face. He punched me in the face and everything went dizzy. I started screaming and he slapped me. The other one told me to stop and they should go. They let go of me and I slid down the wall."

Vickie, "Son of a b."

John looks over Vickie as he can see a transformation happening. "Vickie?"

Vickie, "How did you get back?"

Cindy holds her hand over her mouth and cries as Vickie pulls her hand away.

Vickie quietly asks, "What happened next?"

Cindy gulps. "I don't know how long I sat there but I managed to get back up and walked back here. After a few minutes, you guys showed up."

Vickie, "It has only been a few minutes? Was one wearing a leather jacket with a sport logo on it?"

Cindy, "I don't know, yes. The one that hit me."

Vickie starts to leave when John asks, "Vick, what are you doing?"

Vickie, "Take care of her, John."

John, "Wait, Vickie, we need to call the police."

Vickie goes down the hall. "Call them." Vickie approaches the alleyway where she remembered two suspicious characters stayed at one time and offered her drugs. She is sure they are the same men. As she goes down the dark alley, two men stand up from behind a dumpster. It is the same ones who approached Vickie long ago. One with a leather jacket stands in front of her. "Well, well, what do we have here? Wait, I remember you. You come back to party."

Vickie, "I come for my friend you beat the hell out of tonight."

The man responds. "That bitch spit an expensive gift I gave her."

Vickie spits in his face; as the man wipes his face off says, "You will pay for that!" He begins to throw a punch as Vickie hits him with both fists meeting at both sides of his head near the temples. His eyes roll in a stunned look and drops to the ground limp.

The other puts his hands up. "No problem, okay?"

Vickie walks over fast and grabs him by his shirt and at that time a police car pulls up with lights on all them.

Police command, "Everyone stop!" The police arrest both men as they take a statement from Vickie.

Police officer, "You were lucky, young lady. They could have hurt you bad like your friend."

Vickie begins to walk away. "No, they couldn't." Vickie arrives back at her dorm room and John is waiting for her. Vickie, "Where is Cindy?"

John, "Paramedics took her to a hospital and police have already been here. What did you do?"

"The police arrested the two men."

"You found them?"

"Yes."

"I have to ask, did you do anything to them?"

Vickie looks intently at John. "They got off light."

"Are you okay?"

"I am fine. Go home."

"Okay, try to rest okay." John leaves as Vickie goes to the bathroom and stares at herself in the mirror.

The next morning, Vickie gets ready to go to the hospital to check on Cindy. At that moment, a knock on her door sounds out. She opens and a school campus police officer says, "Vickie Newsome. I am Officer Johnson and this is Deputy Sims from the sheriff's office."

Vickie motions them in. As they walk in, the sheriff asks, "Ma'am, have a couple of questions about last night."

Vickie sits down on Cindy's bed as the two officers stand.

Deputy, "You discovered Ms. Jones beat up and then you questioned her on the whereabouts of the two suspects.

Then you went looking for these men and upon finding them, engaged them in a fight. Is that correct?"

Vickie looks at the deputy. "I had seen these two men before, and I went to find them so I could call the police to arrest them."

The deputy smiles and takes his hat off to kneel next to Vickie. "I have been doing this for a long time. The last thing we need is a vigilante. I know you are tough, I can see it. You could have got yourself killed and instead of investigating a battery case, we could be working a homicide right now. You might think you know what you are doing but let me tell you something, young lady, you don't. Anything can happen in confrontations. It can go bad in no time. Understand?"

Vickie stares for a moment. "That can happen anytime to any of us."

Deputy has a more serious look on his face. "That is true. But when you go after people like that, it makes you the bad person."

Vickie, "Sometimes we have no choice to be what is considered wrong to make things right."

The deputy exhales and stands up. He puts his hat on and turns toward the door. "You got away with it this time." The deputy turns and looks at Vickie. "Better not happen again."

Vickie just stares sternly at the deputy. The deputy looks back. "Ma'am." He leaves as the campus officer follows closing the door.

Vickie arrives at Cindy's hospital room to find Cindy talking to her parents.

Cindy says, "Mom, Dad, this is my roommate Vickie."

Cindy's mom, "We saw her last year we stopped by remember."

Cindy says, "Oh yea."

Cindy's mom hugs Vickie. "Thank you for taking care of my little girl."

Vickie, "All I did was find her, it was my boyfriend John that helped her."

Cindy's dad, "No, you took care of those two criminals."

Cindy says, "Dad!"

Dad responds, "Well, that is what they are. I heard you hurt one of them really bad, the one that hurt my cinnamon."

Vickie, "He tried to strike me. That was a bad mistake on his part."

Dad, "Good."

The parents step outside the room as Vickie approaches the bed. "How are you, roomy?"

Cindy, "I will be out of here tomorrow. They were going to let me out of here today but mom insists they observe me another day."

Vickie laughs.

Cindy, "Vickie, thank you. When I heard you got those guys I felt so relieved."

"There was no way I was going to let those guys get away with it."

Cindy starts to cry as Vickie says, "It is okay, Cin."

"They hurt me bad. I have never been through anything like that. Have you?"

"No. I went through something much different."

Cindy changes from self-pity to concern. "Tell me about it sometime, I know you don't like talking about your past."

Vickie smiles and grabs Cindy's hand. "I promise."

Cindy smiles as her parents come back in.

Vickie stands up. "Well, I will let you guys spend time with each other. Cindy, see you tomorrow."

Cindy, "Don't eat all my snacks."

Vickie smiles as she gives hugs to her mom and shakes hands with her dad.

Earning Your Stripes

V ICKIE MANAGES TO go to one class while Cindy spends one last day in the hospital. John meets up with her for lunch.

John, "How is Cindy?"

Vickie, "She is fine, just going to be bruised for a while. She will be wearing sunglasses for a while."

"She seems to anyway, you know like she is hiding."

They both laugh as they eat sandwiches.

John, "It really scared me that you went after those guys. At the same time, I hoped you would do something bad to them. Is that bad of me?"

Vickie, "Are you kidding? I am the one who beat one of them up and you are worried about your feelings about it?"

John laughs. "Is kind of stupid, I guess."

"Cindy will be back tomorrow, I will do something nice to welcome her back."

"I will help."

"Thanks, John."

They finish lunch and Vickie attends several afternoon classes and then prepares for her martial arts evening class. During her class, Sato has continually stared at her. This is the evening she stays after with him to study Aikido after karate is over. As everyone leaves, Sato walks up with brown paper with something in it.

Vickie, "Sensei, I am so sorry for what I did. I know you have heard what happened."

Sato raises his hand, "It is okay."

Vickie takes a deep breath.

Sato, "What you did would not be considered smart by most."

Vickie, "I know, but something took over and I had to get those guys."

Sato smiles. "In this so-called 'modern age' we have laws that govern almost every action we do. But the reality of life remains constant. There will always be predators, victims, and protectors." He opens the paper and lays in it is an old black belt that has embroidered on it a tiger. "This is the first belt I ever got. My sensei had it made for me and called me the tiger. I want you to have it."

"I can't take that."

"It would be my honor that you wear it."

Vickie picks up the belt and looks at it.

"You are the tiger that protects. No matter where you are and what you become in life, you will always be this."

Vickie's eyes became huge as she looks at Sato and bows. Sato bows back.

Vickie wakes up as Cindy breaks into the room saying, "Oh my God. I love my parents but I am so glad they are gone. They had those doctors running every test known to man on me."

Vickie laughs. "You look good."

Cindy stops. "Are you kidding? I look like an abused wife."

"I got you a present, well, John and I did."

Cindy sits down and opens the box to find a whistle. She picks it up. "Really, a whistle."

"In case you get in trouble again. Look under the paper it was on."

Cindy lifts the paper, and there is a necklace with a strange amulet with Japanese characters. "What does this say?"

"It means loosely, 'I can endure all.'"

Cindy gives Vickie a hug. "I love it." Cindy goes back to her bed. "Now, you did not eat my snacks, did you?"

"No, your snacks would kill me. But I did get you some cookies on your shelf there."

"Thank you."

"When will you be going back to class?"

"I need to give it a few days and I am seeing a counselor. I am still shaken up but will be okay. Can I ask you a question, Vickie?"

Vickie nods yes.

"If the police did not show up, what would you have done?"

"Let's put it this way, they would have not been walking well for a long time." Vickie starts to laugh as Cindy joins in.

"You know, I thought all this martial art stuff was obsessive and even dangerous, but now I see how it is good."

"Cindy, you are right, it is obsessive and is dangerous. Well, to the wrong people it is dangerous."

"Thank you for defending me."

"You're welcome. Well, I guess I better get my day started seeing someone woke me so early."

"Sorry I just had to get out of that place as soon as possible."

Vickie arrives that evening to settle in for a quiet evening while Cindy sits eating the cookies she was given.

"Want one?"

"No thanks."

Vickie reads a book as Cindy stares at her.

"Vickie, you have a promise to make good."

Vickie flips a page. "What is that?"

"Your past."

Vickie stops reading and slowly closes the book. "Okay." Vickie sits up. "My dad was a mean drunk. It seemed he could not control himself unless someone was there to give him parental care. He never touched me but used to beat my mom."

Cindy, "Oh my goodness, sorry I made that comment earlier about an abused woman."

"Don't worry. Anyway, Mom had to tell me the stories because I was young and I don't remember everything exactly. I guess maybe I have blocked it some. But my dad was hitting my mom and I got his gun and pointed at him."

Cindy covers her mouth and starts to tear up.

Vickie, "He cleaned up in rehab. He was really good, for a while. He was not as bad as before and Mom learned to speak up against him. But he did continue to drink. He would just say hurtful things to us, mainly mom. What got me through was my cousin who was grown. He was almost like a brother to my dad, they were close in age. My cousin had long talks with me and let me look through his telescope. I like astronomy back then."

Cindy, "Sounds like a nice guy."

Vickie, "He was. He always seemed to be. When I became a teenager, he was always there to help. I spent weeks at a time over his family's house when things got bad at home. They always seem bad. When I was sixteen, one day my cousin and I were alone and he tried to seduce me. I turned him away but later he drugged me and raped me."

Cindy, "Oh my God!"

Vickie chokes a bit. "I was pregnant and my mom insisted that dad should know then. My dad—in an alcoholic rage—called me and my mom, you know, and stormed out the house with his gun. My cousin was waiting for him and shot my dad dead. When the dust settled, my mom changed. It was like she died too when my dad did."

Cindy, "What about your kid?"

Vickie looks up at Cindy as Cindy says. "I'm sorry."

"No, it is okay. Mom made me give my child up for adoption. I felt like an empty shell. Then I had a teacher named Mr. Sanders who helped me deal with it all. When therapist did not work, he reached me. He is the whole reason I am here today."

"I am so sorry, Vickie. I didn't know you had went through all that? What happened to your cousin?"

"It was ruled self-defense but he got in trouble for other things. They found the illegal drugs he used to drug me."

"What about the rape?"

"What about it? We never pushed it. Mom could not live with the shame and I was too out it to care anymore."

"He got away with it?"

"Not exactly but legally yes." Vickie walks around a bit and then picks up a picture of her mother. "My mom died of a heart attack later and tried to apologize for everything."

"I don't even know where to begin. Your cousin, parents, and losing your kid, oh my God!"

"It was incredible."

"How does anyone survive something like that?"

"I almost didn't. If Mr. Sanders had not made a difference."

Cindy starts crying. "It is all so horrible."

Vickie sits down next to her and puts her arm around Cindy.

Cindy, "You are comforting me. My God you wear it like a badge of honor."

Vickie, "I am fine, really."

"There is no way you can be fine. You just can't. I am seeing someone and I just got beat up compared to what you have."

"Cindy, please understand that I am stronger than my pain."

"I hope so because I would sure hate for that dam to break."

Vickie goes back to reading her book smiling. Cindy leans back grabbing her cookies and staring at Vickie in disbelief.

Dear John

 IT IS THE middle of the school year, and John and Vickie have been an item around campus going everywhere and doing everything together it seems. All seems right in the world. They are walking around the park not much said to each for a while.

John finally breaks the silence. "Vickie, do you ever think about getting married someday?"

Vickie laughs. "Are you proposing?"

John quickly and nervously says, "No, no, not all. I am just talking hypothetically. I think about it sometimes."

Vickie. "Well, I really have not considered it especially since I am working on college."

"True, college gives us enough to think about. But after is what I am talking about. I know I am not a typical guy but I really like the idea of career, being married, even kids."

"That is nice, maybe you are looking for stability and those concepts are the most perceived stable."

John looks at Vickie. "Maybe."

Vickie holds John's hand as John says, "I like you, Vickie. I like you a lot."

"I like you too."

"You think you would ever feel any more serious about me than like?"

Vickie is quiet looking at the ground for a minute and then stops to face John.

Vickie, "You are a very cool guy, and I like you a lot. I can see myself someday maybe even loving you. You have to understand, John, that I am not sure what love is anymore. I have been through so much that I am worried I could not give you or anyone the stability that you are seeking."

"Whatever you have been through I am not afraid of it. You are one of the most stable people I have ever met. Something is so different about you. It is like your mind is much older than many. It is hard to pin down. I have strong feelings for you."

"Are you sure it is just not some need you have? Maybe you just replaced your drinking for me."

John looks dismayed. "I am in love with you, Vickie, there I said it. I fell in love with you the first day you were carrying your stuff to your room."

Vickie's eyes became wide looking at John up and down his face.

John, "I love you, Vickie, and always will. I can't think of another girl I would want to be with." John stares at her as Vickie looks confused. Suddenly, she grabs John's head and kisses him passionately. John says, "Wow, I feel almost dizzy. Does that mean you love me too?"

Vickie, "It might be wrong but maybe I do. There is something about you, John, that draws me to you. I never thought I would ever feel this way. But when I am with you I feel protective of you and at the same time defenseless."

John kisses Vickie as they find a park bench and begin to passionately kiss each other.

Vickie returns to her room, and Cindy says, "Where have you been?"

Vickie, "Out with John."

Cindy, "You look different."

Vickie wipes her mouth. "How do you mean?"

"I don't know, like almost happy."

Vickie sits on the bed. "John told me he loves me."

"Oh my God, really. He is a nice guy. What did you tell him?"

"I think I am in love with him."

"I am so happy for you. You deserve it so much."

"It is not about deserving but about being practical. I don't have time for a boyfriend."

"Oh stop. Let yourself be happy."

"Is that your prescription, doctor?"

"Listen to a psychologist in the making."

Vickie lies down on her bed staring at the ceiling.

Cindy, "You could do a lot worse."

Vickie, "I could do a lot better too. Should I be satisfied with the middle?"

"You are such an optimist."

Vickie laughs.

A few days later, Vickie goes out with John. They drive to a secluded area and begin to be passionate. After a bit, John holds a ring in front of Vickie.

Vickie, "What's this, John?"

John, "A promise ring."

Vickie pushes his hand with the ring back saying, "John, please don't."

"I'm sorry."

"Don't be sorry, it is just overwhelming to me."

"I am being too pushy, I know. I am just so afraid of losing you."

"That is very honest and I appreciate it. You are not going to lose me."

"I just feel like that sometimes."

"Is there something that is making you worried?"

John gulps. "No, not at all. I just love you so much."

John looks down at the ring as Vickie looks at the ring and back up at John. She moves his head to her and kisses him.

Vickie, "Relax."

John smiles and puts the ring in his pocket. Vickie smiles and they spend the evening kissing and holding each other. Their passion grows as the weeks pass.

They decide to go to a carnival, and as they ride the rides, Kevin shows up with his date and they all spend the evening together. Kevin's date comes back with four beers. She offers the two extra to John and Vickie as Vickie says, "None for me, thanks."

John grabs one. "It has been a long time but I think I am due."

Vickie and Kevin look at John, as he responds, "Just one for old time's sake."

They don't argue and the evening continues fine with loads of fun. As Vickie and John are walking back to her dorm.

John, "What is wrong?"

Vickie, "When did you start drinking again?"

"I just had one tonight because they had extra."

"I am not stupid, John, she brought those because you had been drinking and she knew it. That is your roommate and his date."

John, "Okay you got me, I have been drinking casually."

Vickie, "That is a problem, John."

"Okay, you win, I quit again."

Vickie shakes her head in disgust as she walks away. "Vickie!"

John just looks concerned but leaves.

Next day, Cindy and Vickie are having lunch when John sits down.

"Hey ladies."

Cindy, "Hey, John, how are you?"

John, "I am good, Cindy. How are you, Vick?"

Vickie looks at him. "John."

Cindy looks back and forth at both of them. "Are you two fighting?"

John, "I had a beer last night at the carnival, and Vickie is not happy about it."

Vickie, "One, what about all the others?"

John, "I know you have issues with drinking but I am who I am."

Cindy, "I am gonna go now."

Vickie, "Stay, Cindy. John, you know…you know what? Go be John then."

John, "Are you saying we are done?"

Vickie, "Can't get anything past you."

John gets up. "You know, Vickie, never mind."

John walks off as Cindy says, "really, girl?"

Vickie, "I can't be with a drunk."

Cindy looks at Vickie who is not eating now. "You okay, Vickie?"

Vickie looks up with heavy eyes. "Yes, I am fine."

"C'mon, you, me girls' night out. No martial arts, no boys, just us girls."

"Okay."

Night hits and Cindy and Vickie go out for a nice dinner. They see a movie and walk around the campus grounds.

Vickie, "It doesn't scare you walking around at night?"

Cindy, "Not while you are with me."

"You know, I could teach you some good lessons on self-defense."

"You have before."

"Yea, but you have to practice it. You have to build the neuromuscular memory so it is almost instinct."

"How about I just hang around you more."

Vickie grabs her arm. "Okay, girly."

They go back to their dorm room and sit on Cindy's bed.

Vickie, "I had a good time, thank you."

Cindy, "Thank you for protecting me."

Vickie smiles as Cindy gives her a kiss on the cheek.

Vickie, "Okay, thank you."

Cindy leans over to slowly kiss her as Vickie pulls away and stands up.

Cindy, "I'm sorry."

Vickie, "No, it is okay. I didn't know."

"I'm sorry I just felt…I did not mean anything by it."

"No, it is okay." Vickie goes into the bathroom and stares at the mirror. She mumbles to herself, "What is wrong with me?" After a while, Vickie comes out and lies in bed. Cindy is facing away in her bed.

"Vickie."

"What?"

"I'm sorry I made a pass at you."

"That is okay, I did not know you were lesbian."

"Nobody knows."

"I don't care, Cindy, I just am not interested okay."

Cindy turns over, "Okay, but I just feel bad because so many have taken advantage of and here I am at a low point in your life."

"That is nothing. I do not even see any issue. Don't worry about it okay."

"I love you, Vickie, and I mean platonically."

"I love you too, Cindy. You are a good friend. You had me fooled, your parents know."

"Mom knows and she is okay with it. Dad would never understand."

"Yea, dads."

Cindy looks at Vickie and feels sad for bringing up issues relating to her past.

Junior Minced

ANOTHER YEAR AT college has come, and Vickie has been excelling in grades and accomplishments. She is head of several groups as business leaders and future executives. Cindy and Vickie have remained close friends as Cindy keeps trying to hook Vickie up with guys. John has continued drinking and his jealousy of Vickie continues to grow into a deep obsession. Meanwhile, Vickie has reached a third-degree black belt in karate and continues vigilantly to better her abilities. She spends another night of teaching karate and starts her evening of Aikido. Sensei Sato has two other people that night that have dressed up for the evening's Aikido lessons. Vickie is wondering who the other two are.

Sensei Sato greets her, "Ms. Newsome, these two men are associates of mine and they have come to test you. Are you okay with that?"

Vickie bows. "Of course, Sensei."

The first man comes up and squares off with Vickie. He moves quick but gracefully as Vickie tries to avoid his snares and catches. After a few minutes, he manages to bring her down and then lets her up. He bows and she bows back as he sits down. The next man stands up and bows to Vickie and she bows. He simply stands there as she slowly moves toward him. She tries grabs onto his Keikogi which is the Aikido top part of the uniform. She tries to gain leverage to move him but his hands never leave their side as everything she attempts simply moves herself off balance. The man never raises his hands to defend himself even when Vickie tries to kick him; he seems to move forward pushing her over with his body. She manages to stay on her feet. She then spins around in the air to try to kick him in the top part of his chest, and she feels nothing touch her as she lands on her side almost upside down. She jumps back up and the man is sitting in the chair with the others. She stands up and the man stands and bows to her as she bows back. He sits down as Sato looks at both and they nod yes. Sato gets up and bows to Vickie and she bows back.

Sato, "You have been promoted to Shodan."

Vickie is humbled as this means she has reached the equivalent of first degree black belt in Aikido. She bows at Sato and the two men stand up and bow to her as she bows back. The men leave to change as Vickie asks Sato, "Sensei, who are they?"

Sato looks back at the dressing room door and replies, "Let's just say you were evaluated by two men who personally trained under the master who invented Aikido. Vickie is humbled as she has an idea of who they are. Sato, "They don't come for anyone. Only those who carry the spirit of this art in its true way. Next, we will begin teaching you Kendo, the way of the sword."

Vickie, "What about Aikido?"

Sato laughs. "Aikido is swords. It is the same techniques without a sword in hand. Everything in Japan revolves around the sword."

Vickie bows as Sato bows back.

Vickie is having lunch on campus and Kevin asks, "May I join you?"

Vickie, "Of course, silly."

Kevin sits down next to Vickie and asks, "Have not seen you in a while since you and John split up."

"Yea, John."

"It is none of my business but you know John is still pining for you."

"You here to agent for him?"

"No, not me. Just wondering if you still like him."

"Of course I like him but I can't be with him."

"Drinking, I know. I am sorry he has a problem with it. To be honest, it has got really bad recently. We have found him passed out several times in the last few weeks on the grounds."

"John."

"You know, he and I were high school friends too."

"No, I did not. I wondered why you guys were so thick from the freshman year." Vickie looks around for a bit and asks, "Say are you still with that girl from the carnival?"

Kevin, "Carnival? Oh her, no. We went out once in a great while but not serious."

"So you are available."

Kevin laughs. "Yes totally available. Especially for you."

Vickie smiles. "So you want to go out sometime?"

"Isn't that my line?"

"Sorry."

"Don't be, I like that."

They pause and watch people walk by.

Kevin, "You are quite popular in the biz groups."

Vickie, "They are politically important for resumes."

"Ah, thinking ahead. What are your goals?"

"Career wise, I want to run a large company. Govern my own destiny and have the financial independence to live as I want."

"You and everyone else on this planet. You have a road map to get there?"

"I have a few ideas."

"Care to share?"

Vickie looks at Kevin and smirks. "I plan to intern as a junior executive in a marketing company. That gives me access to other companies and get an idea of their plans and which direction they are heading to. This gives me an idea of what to invest in. Eventually, I hope to have enough investment capital built to buy my way into high-level executive positions somewhere."

"Wow. Okay, that is interesting."

"That sound workable?"

"Sounds like you lived a life already in business and just following what you did before."

"Your funny, it is just logical."

"Hey, I have to run, you want to go out tonight?"

"Yea, that would be fine, I have no class tonight."

"I will meet you at the front of your dorm at seven."

"See you there."

Kevin smiles and walks off.

Vickie smiles to herself and finishes her lunch.

Kevin arrives at Vickie's dorm, and Vickie comes out on queue it seems.

Vickie, "Hi, handsome."

Kevin, "Hey, beautiful."

They hold hands and walk to the parking lot in front of Kevin's frat house to get his car. As they walk away, out of the shadows, John steps out to watch them. He drinks his beer and walks distantly behind them. Kevin and Vickie get in his card and head to a drive in burger joint.

Kevin, "This okay?"

Vickie, "It is fine."

"What do you want?"

"I would love a fish sandwich and vanilla shake."

"Good choice."

Kevin orders their food and looks at Vickie. "So here we are."

Vickie, "Yes, here we are."

Kevin reaches over to kiss Vickie. Vickie looks at him and gives him a kiss. It was a passionless kiss. Kevin leans back to his seat. "Okay then."

Vickie, "Sorry, I guess I have things on my mind."

Kevin exhales. "John."

"Look I am sorry. I guess I still have feelings for him."

They both look down at the dash, as Vickie says, "You know what is weird about it all?"

Kevin looks at her and nods his head no.

"I can't stand to be with him because of his excessive drinking. But for some reason, I can't help but think and feel something for him."

"That is weird. You know what, let us have our food and take you back home."

"I am sorry I am a sucky date."

"No, you are great. It is just that he is my good friend, and I feel a little strange being with the girl who has feelings for him. Also he is obsessed with you."

"You are a very cool guy, Kevin."

He smiles as food arrives. They enjoy a cool evening of food, and Kevin takes her back to the driveway by the dorm. No words were said on the travel as Vickie gets out. "I had a good time Kevin."

Kevin, "So did I."

"Hope you have a good rest of the evening."

"Evening is still young, so I think I will run up to the study hall. For some reason, the silence there helps me think."

Vickie arrives in her room, and Cindy says, "Vickie, you are here."

Vickie, "What's wrong?"

"John was here drunk wanting to know where you and Kevin went to."

"Oh Lord. Where is he now?"

About that moment, a loud sporadic knock comes from the door.

Vickie, "John, you're drunk, get in here."

Vickie grabs John and pulls him in the dorm room.

John, "So you and Kevin have a good time?"

Vickie, "John, you need coffee and a good night's rest."

"Where did you two go?"

Vickie grabs his beer and is about to pour it as she sniffs the opening. "This isn't beer. This is hard liquor. You have a much bigger problem than I thought."

Vickie pours the contents of his beer bottle out into the sink.

John says, "I have more in my room."

Vickie looks disgusted. "John, sit down on my bed and relax."

"I want to know how you feel about Kevin!"

Cindy, "Ah, I think I am going to leave for a bit okay."

Vickie, "Go."

Cindy leaves as Vickie walks up to John. "If you don't stop this, you will regret it. When you sober up, you are going to hate yourself."

"I love you, Vickie, don't you know that. You are all I want in life."

"I love you too, John, but not like this. I am going to call your friend Kevin to come take you back to your room."

"Oh, you are going to call that punk who calls me his friend while he takes my girlfriend."

Vickie holds the phone up, as John is crying. "I wanted to marry you."

"John sweetie, let me get you help."

Vickie dials the study hall as John sits on the bed holding his head in his hands crying constantly. Vickie on the phone with Kevin. "Kevin, John is here in my dorm room. Can you come and pick him up?"

Kevin responds, "Crap, on my way."

Vickie hangs up the phone and sits next to John. "Kevin is on his way."

John, "I really screwed up, didn't I?" Then John's demeanor changes to anger as he stands up. "You witch cheated on me. I am going to my room."

Vickie, "You know what, John, I am done with trying to help you!"

John opens the door chanting obscenities as he leaves. Vickie sits on her bed holding her head in her hands.

Cindy returns. "You just going to let him go?"

Vickie has tears in her eyes. "I can't deal with that. It is too much like my dad."

"What if he gets in trouble?"

"Let him, he needs a wakeup call. He is going to his room."

"You sure?"

Vickie gets up and goes to the bathroom. "I don't care."

John staggers to his frat house parking lot and gets in his car. He backs out hitting two cars and scrapes another driving forward. He heads to the main road out the campus area as he sees the headlights of Kevin oncoming. It is unmistakable because Kevin has extra lights in the middle of his grille. John hits the gas and tries to maintain a straight driving as possible. As soon as Kevin approaches, Kevin is totally unaware of John oncoming. As soon as they are close, John veers toward Kevin hitting him head on. John is ejected from his seat through the windshield and thrown over Kevin's car into the ditch on the side of the road. Kevin's car lifts up as his head hits the steering wheel, killing him instantly. The night grows quiet as the commotion of impact settles down.

Vickie answers the bathroom door as Cindy says, "I think something happened outside. There was a loud crash."

Vickie steps out and goes out her dorm room door. At that moment, the sounds of sirens in the distance invade the silence. Vickie runs downstairs followed by Cindy. Vickie sees police lights reaching an accident down the road as she runs to it. By the time she reaches it, policemen have already set a parameter and stop her. Police, "Young lady, please stay back." Vickie looks over and sees the smashed-in face of Kevin lying lifeless. Police on the other side yell out, "Here is the other one." Shortly after, an ambulance arrives and begins to work on John. Vickie is crying as she sees them loading John on a gurney and into an ambulance. Cindy makes it finally to Vickie totally out of breath. "Is that John?"

Vickie looks at Cindy crying and shakes her head yes. Cindy sees Kevin in his car as the paramedic looks at police shaking his head no to indicate he is gone. Cindy starts tearing up. "Kevin?" Vickie stands straight and starts walking back to her dorm. Cindy looks back and forth between the accident and Vickie and then starts to follow Vickie. Cindy wants to talk but she just walks by Vickie as Vickie stares at the ground whimpering all the way back to the dorm.

They reach the dorm room and Vickie goes in the bathroom and slams the door closed. Cindy feels sorrowful as she says, "Vickie, honey are you okay?" Cindy sits on her bed and says, "Vickie, it is not your fault. Please come out and talk to me." The bathroom door opens as Cindy stands. Vickie is standing for a moment in the doorway then walks briskly toward Cindy and hugs her tight crying.

Cindy, "It's okay. It's okay. I am here."

Vickie and Cindy sit on her bed continuing to hold each other as Vickie cries as if she has been wanting to cry like that for years. The night ends as Vickie lets out event after event of frustration on Cindy's shoulders in the form of tears.

Love is Blond

J OHN IS UNCONSCIOUS in the hospital while Vickie watches. It has been days and Vickie keeps a vigil in his room. She is awoken by a nurse. "Miss, you need to go home."

Vickie, "I am sorry, I drifted off."

The nurse is about to leave when Vickie asks, "Has his parents been here?"

The nurse turns back, "Honey, they are paying for the care but have not been here."

"They know he is here but have not been here."

"Look, I don't know the details but the rumor is they won't see him because he killed someone while drinking."

Vickie gives a disgusted look as the nurse leaves. She stares at John and walks over to his bedside. John is on a respirator with IVs feeding him solution.

Vickie holds John, "I should have kept you with me. I am so sorry, John. I love you." Vickie wipes the tears from her face and places his hand comfortably to his side and leaves.

Vickie arrives back at her dorm and Cindy wakes up; "Hey, Vickie, what time is it?"

"Two a.m."

"Oh, good night."

"Good night, Cin."

The next morning, Cindy wakes up for class and Vickie is already gone. Cindy goes to the hospital and finds Vickie staring at John. "Vickie, I did not even hear you leave."

Vickie, "I did not want to wake you again."

Cindy walks over to John. "Has he come to any?"

"No."

"Do they know when he will come out of it?"

"It could be days, even years."

Cindy looks at John. "My God. Vickie, why don't you let me watch him and you go rest."

"I did this to him, I can't leave."

"Oh, Vick, please don't do this to yourself." Cindy sits down in the chair next to John and Vickie looks back at John. A few minutes later, Sato arrives. Vickie stands up and bows as Sato says, "Please, Ms. Newsome, no need for formalities here. I wanted to check on you."

"Sensei…"

"Please Sato or Mr. Takashi."

"Mr. Takashi, I am sorry for missing class."

"No need to apologize. I heard about the accident and I am sorry."

"I should have never let him leave."

Sato looks at John and back at Vickie. "Let me ask you a question, Ms. Newsome. You cannot control everything around you in life. He made his choice long before he ever took a drink. His collision was just a matter of time. Blaming yourself only validates that which is not true. Feel sorry for him but you did not make this happen."

"Thank you, Mr. Takashi."

Sato nods to Cindy and walks to the door and says, "They did it to themselves. All of them." Sato looks at Vickie as she looks back confused that he somehow knows her past. Or maybe he can just see it in her. Sato, "Insulate yourself from the world, never isolate. Understand, Ms. Newsome?"

Vickie nods yes. Sato nods back and smiles as he leaves. Cindy and Vickie look at each other as Vickie sits down.

Cindy, "Are you going to Kevin's funeral tomorrow?"

Vickie, "Can you watch John if I go?"

"Of course, Vick."

"Thank you, Cin."

The next day, Cindy arrives at the hospital as Vickie is dressed up in a black dress.

Cindy, "Vickie, there is a cab waiting to take you to the funeral. After it will bring you back, my parents paid for it."

Vickie, "Thank you, Cindy, and thank your parents for it."

Vickie holds John's hand. "I will be back, John." Vickie slowly leaves to the cab. The cab arrives at the funeral as Kevin's family lives in the town the college is in. Vickie stands at the back of the family and friends of the gravesite. Everyone stares at the casket as Kevin's mother sees Vickie and walks back to her. Vickie is holding back tears as her eyes are full of sympathy. Kevin's mom grabs Vickie's hand and says, "Be with us." She leads Vickie to the front with the family. The priest commences the final ceremonies and the casket is lowered. Vickie cannot control the tears as Kevin's mom hands her a tissue.

Vickie, "Thank you, Mrs. Lesterson."

Mrs. Lesterson, "He loved John. They were friends since they were waist-high to me. I forgive John but I don't forgive you. The reason I don't forgive you is there is nothing to forgive. I know you have been watching John at the hospital. Please, if I could forgive John for what he did to my baby, you can forgive yourself." Vickie weeps as she looks at Mr. Lesterson and he nods yes to her. "Vickie, go and do what my son told me you were meant to do in this world. The world needs you. Strong people who can make a difference. Kevin believed that about you. He knew it and he even preached it to us. He saw in you something he never has seen in anyone else. Don't let his belief in you die in vain. Please don't, for my son's sake."

Vickie, "I promise, I will. I will."

The family start to leave as Vickie looks back at the casket in the hole.

Vickie, "Kevin, I will." Vickie leaves to her cab and it takes her back to the hospital.

Vickie arrives and Cindy is reading a magazine.

Cindy, "How are you?"

Vickie, "I am fine, Cin. Let's go."

"What about John?"

"I will visit him from time to time but I have a life to live. The meteor hit but I am still alive."

Cindy looks confused as they both walk out. "What meteor?"

"I will tell you later."

A couple of days later, Vickie comes back from martial arts class, and Cindy says, "Vickie, the hospital called, John is awake now."

Vickie, "Thanks, Cin."

"Wait, coming with you."

"That is okay, I am fine."

Vickie arrives at the hospital and John is barely awake. She holds his hand, "Hey, Johnny."

John very weak sounding, "Hey, Vickie, why am I here? They told me I was in an accident."

Vickie, "Yes you were. You were asleep for days."

"Is my car totaled?"

"Yes. What do you remember?"

"Nothing."

"You just rest, John."

"Vickie, thank you for being here. I did not think you liked me anymore."

"John, I have always loved you. You rest now."

John falls asleep again as Vickie stares.

The next day, Vickie arrives in John's room, and he is more lucid than before.

"Vickie, you were here last night. I did not imagine that right?"

"Yes I was here. I have been here every day watching you till you woke up."

John smiles. "That makes me feel good. Can you do me a favor?"

"Sure, John."

"Can you let Kevin know I am awake."

Vickie looks at the ground and then to the window with tears in her eyes.

John asks, "What's wrong?"

"John, this is hard for you to hear but Kevin and you were in an accident."

"What? Is he okay?"

"You were drunk the night of the accident and upset I was out with Kevin. I called Kevin to come back and get you and you stormed mad out my dorm room. I thought you were going back to your frat house. Instead you got in your car and wrecked it, leaving the parking lot against a few cars. You were really drunk, and down the Ella Street, you saw Kevin coming in the other lane. For some reason, you hit him head on. The accident threw you through the windshield."

John has tears rolling down him cheek. "What about Kevin?" He repeats angrily and upset, "What about Kevin?"

"He died in the accident."

John turns his head the other way and starts crying. "Kevin…Kevin."

Vickie stands up and holds John's hand. "John, look at me."

John turns to Vickie with his eyes full of watery tears.

"You have to let this go."

"How can I? I killed my best friend in the world."

"I know. I blamed myself too but Kevin's family told me they forgave you. If they can forgive you, then you can forgive yourself. I know you don't feel that way now but you must start thinking about it."

"I don't deserve to live."

"Kevin loved you, please live for him."

About that time, an accident detective for the sheriff's office comes in. "Ma'am, are you related to him?"

"I am, I am his girlfriend."

Detective, "I understand, I need to ask him some questions, can you leave us?"

Vickie looks down at John. "I love you, John, I will be back later okay."

John nods his head yes as Vickie smiles and walks to the door where the detective is. She stops and whispers to the detective, "Please be nice to him, he just found out what happened."

Detective, "I just have some simple questions to ask."

Vickie, "I know you are gathering evidence to charge him with the death of his best friend. Remember, it was his best friend."

"Young lady, you need to leave."

Vickie turns and stares into his eyes and he stares back.

Detective, "It will be all right."

Vickie nods okay as she leaves.

The Forgiver

VICKIE VISITS WITH John who is still recovering in the hospital. She pulls a chair next to John's bed and holds his hand.

Vickie, "How are you doing, John?"

John, "Considering I killed my best friend, lost my girlfriend, injured my body badly, parents ashamed of me, being an alcoholic, and probably going to jail as well as my career being over, I am okay."

"Well, when you put it like that, it sounds bad."

John frowns as Vickie says, "Look, this is an opportunity to start over. You kick the drinking habit, you face your legal issues, and then get your life back on track. You can still finish college and have a good career."

"I don't see how."

"If you would have told me that I would be in college as a young teenager, I would have laughed you out the room.

There was no hope for me. Life just keeps moving along and you just have to get back in the flow."

"I don't want to live anymore."

"I didn't either long ago. I wanted to die so many times. For some reason, I kept chasing the carrot. There was always someone who believes in me. Just one person believing in me at the right times made the difference. Got me to a point where I could stand on my own feet. John, I believe in you."

"Not enough to be with me."

"I am here now. I do love you, John. You are the most interesting and wonderful guy I know. But when you drink, I see my dad and that is a pain I can't live with. Can you understand that?"

"Actually, yes I can. I thought before the accident that you just needed to get over it. I realize now that it is not that simple."

"Getting over it is an excuse that people not having the same issues say. They really do not understand trauma. It is easy for people who have not gone through truly tough times to know what it is like to live after a traumatic event. Now you are and see what I am talking about."

"That is for sure."

"John, look at me, you will get through this. I am not leaving your side. We may not be meant for each other, I don't even know if there is such a thing. But I will help you through this crisis."

"I appreciate that. My parents are getting the best lawyers to defend me. They seem to think I can get away with probation. But I am out the fraternity and maybe in the school."

"At least you are getting good help legally. You are not getting away with anything. You will have to live with this the rest of your life. There is no punishment that can equal that in the end. But you must live on."

"Yea, live on, whatever that is?"

Vickie looks down at the ground and then back up. "You know what killed the dinosaurs?"

"What? An asteroid, I guess."

"No, that was just the start of things. It was actually the lack of sunlight from the dust and cold that killed the dinosaurs eventually. But even after the meteor hit, they had life. Those that survived the impact still had to carry on. This is your meteor and the dust may cloud your life for years, but you must continue to live. So live your life."

"You sound like a motivational speaker."

"It came from one, the greatest one I know. Live, John, live for me and live for you. Live for those you will help in the future."

John's eyes are heavy with tears as he looks up at Vickie. "You think I can really recover from this?"

"Yes."

Vickie stands up.

"John, call me if you need anything. I will see you tomorrow, okay?"

John nods yes as Vickie leaves and then says, "Vick…I love you."

Vickie, "I love you too, John." She smiles and leaves.

Weeks pass and John has been formally charged in the death of his friend, Kevin. He is able to wheelchair to the courthouse as he attends various legal proceedings. He has managed now to be able to stand and walk with a severe limp. It has been found to have enough evidence to have John face trial. His legal team have prepared well as his court date arrives. His parents, friends, Vickie, and family members of Kevin attend. John is tearful as prosecution describes the accident in detail and police as well as other witnesses give testimony. John can only think of his friend Kevin. Vickie is even called to describe what she saw as well as Cindy. He is found guilty of manslaughter and now is up to the judge to decide his punishment. The judge allows final words from friends and family of John and Kevin. Vickie approaches and begins to address the judge. "Your Honor, I am here not to condone the actions of drinking that caused this accident. My father, excuse me, drank and it was very hard living with that. John, despite his drinking problem, is a good man. It has been an honor to know him. You see I could have stopped him and avoided this whole thing. But I let him go, and this whole terrible event took place.

I wish you to consider that John has many good things to contribute to this world. Please don't incarcerate him where his goodness will stagnate. He needs help, not jail. Help him so he can continue to help others. He volunteers to so many groups to help people with disabilities. I never even knew he did all that. He just kept it a secret. That is the way he is, never brags, just does things that are good. He had one weakness and that weakness caused him to make a terrible mistake. He will have to live with that. Please don't punish the ones who helps for that one mistake. He can't bring back his friend, Kevin, but he can live for him. Thank you, Your Honor."

Vickie sits down as the judge calls for anyone else who would like to speak. He calls again and there is silence. As the judge is about to call an end to this part, Kevin's mom Mrs. Lesterson steps up. "I would like to say something." The judge motions for her to come forward to the podium. Mrs. Lesterson wipes some tears and clears her throat to speak.

"My dear Kevin was taken from me and his father. Taken from us by someone who grew up with Kevin. They met in third grade and did everything together. They shared toys, stories, and their lives. They were like brothers. Kevin loved John and we loved John. They even followed each other into college and even chose similar career paths so they might stay together in work later. John did not kill my boy, alcohol did. If you have to punish anything, punish the demon alcohol for what it to my boy. Get John treatment but let John go. Let him continue the path that he and my boy set out to do. If I can forgive John and want him to live free, you can too, Your Honor. Shouldn't it be me who decides his fate? If there was justice it would be up to me. So I say let him go. Because he is the only son I have left now."

She cries and slowly makes her way back to the seat with the help of her husband. Everyone is teary eyed including the jury. The judge asks John if he would like to make a final statement before sentencing.

John stands up and stares down at the podium. "I'm sorry, Kev. I am sorry, Mr. and Mrs. Lesterson. I am sorry for everyone here and all those I have hurt." John turns around and stands by his lawyer's side as his lawyer puts his hand on John's shoulder.

Silence prevails in the courtroom as the judge writes and scribbles away, sometimes stopping to look around. Then finally, he says, "John Patterson, having been found guilty by a jury of your peers on the charge of manslaughter of Kevin Lesterson, I am sentencing you to probation for six years following a mandatory rehab program for alcohol. Your license is suspended for a period of two years following successful completion of said program and is signed off by an accredited alcohol counselor. Dismissed." The Judge slams the gavel as the courtroom erupts in joy.

John falls back in his chair exhausted. Even the jurors clap their hands happy with the verdict. Vickie runs over and hugs John almost squeezing the air out him.

Mr. and Mrs. Lesterson walk up to John as he stands.

John, "Thank you."

Mrs. Lesterson, "You finish what you and Kevin started, you hear?"

"Yes, ma'am."

"I expect to see you on Thanksgiving after your parents' meal as usual."

"I will be there."

They leave as John is helped by Vickie back to the hospital to continue rest and rehabilitation.

Vickie spends time with John once in a while as his physical rehab coincides with his alcohol addiction rehab. Partly through rehab, one of the counselors meets with Vickie privately.

Counselor, "Vickie, I think it is wonderful you helping John, and he is making a lot of improvements the last few weeks. I need you to do a favor?"

Vickie, "Of course, whatever he needs."

"Good. I need to you leave him alone at least till he is out of rehab."

"What, why?"

"Because you were a weak point at which he drank. He needs to work that issue out, and it would go easier if you were not around."

Vickie looks confused but then shows understanding. "I get it. Should I say good-bye for now?"

"He already knows that I was going to ask you this. He wanted me to tell you that he is okay. Also something about no more meteors."

Vickie laughs. "Okay, I understand."

"Very good. I will contact you when it is all right to meet him again."

Vickie shakes hands with the counselor and leaves the hospital.

Senior Moments

ANOTHER YEAR HAS come and the summer has passed. Cindy returns from her festivities.

Cindy, "Hey girl!" as she hugs Vickie. "Don't you go anywhere? Have you been here all summer?"

Vickie, "Everything I need is a walk away, besides where am I going to go?"

"You could come with me."

"Sorry, I just have so much invested here, besides I need to keep control of what money I have. It is enough with scholarships to pay for college debt-free and buy a car later. Trying to stay on target. Not everyone has generous parents."

"Okay, the parents thing again. Okay, I am lucky but I will never be as smart and beautiful as you."

Vickie smiles. "Thank you but I would trade my life for yours in a heartbeat."

"Have you heard from John?"

"He is out of rehab and moved to another college to finish his degree. I heard that from some mutual acquaintances."

"You still love him, don't you?"

"He was the closest guy I could see myself with. But hey I am young, plenty of time for that."

"I have a surprise."

"Oh."

"I met a girl here on campus right before summer started. I called her over the break and we met up. She is awesome. I think I am in love."

"That is great, Cin."

"She lives at the other end of the dorm. I hope you like her."

"It is only important you like her and she is good to you. I suppose you will want to room with her."

"Hell no, you are my roomy. Besides having her move in with might spoil the magic, right?"

"Right. So when do I meet her?"

"She will stop by as soon as she makes back in, probably tomorrow."

"Okay then."

"I would ask what you did over the summer but I already know."

"Then you are correct."

"God, you are so boring at times. But that is what I love about you."

"I think the term you are looking for is 'stable.'"

"Whatever." Cindy unpacks and unwinds as they both settle in.

The next evening, Cindy and Vickie were reading their studies when a knock on the door occurs. Cindy jumps up and answers the door quick. "Lana!"

Lana, "Cindy!"

They both hug and give each other a kiss.

Cindy, "Lana, meet my roomy Vickie. Vickie, Lana."

Vickie stands up and shakes hands with Lana. Lana looks just like Vickie in many respects: tall, blond, similar eyes.

Lana, "You have a strong grip."

Vickie, "So do you."

Lana, "I run a lot and like to climb."

Vickie, "That will do it."

Cindy and Lana sit on her bed as Vickie sits down on hers.

Cindy, "Lana almost wore me out running one time this summer."

Lana, "I think you did get wore out."

Cindy, "True."

They both kiss and smile.

Vickie, "You two seem to really hit it off."

Lana, "Yea, she is smart and cute."

Cindy, "You are so fit and good looking. Vickie, no offense, you are gorgeous too but not available." Cindy's face turns red. "I mean, I'm sorry."

Lana, "Cindy, don't worry about it, it's cool. I can see how you could go for Vickie but she just does not swing that way."

Vickie, "Yes, I am a guy type of girl."

Lana, "That is a shame."

Vickie, "I don't think so."

Cindy, "Say hey, Lana, how about we go out."

Lana stares at Vickie and says, "Sure, Cindy."

They all get up to leave as Lana moves toward the door but her eyes fixed on Vickie. Vickie stares back as they both leave.

The next day at lunch outside, Cindy and Lana arrive and sit on the bench across from Vickie.

Cindy, "Hey, Vickie girl."

Vickie, "Hey, Cin. Hey, Lana."

Lana, "Sticky Vickie, how are you today?"

Vickie looks back. "Just fine, Lana banana."

Cindy, "C'mon ladies, be nice. Hey, Lana and I were thinking of a movie tonight, join us? My treat."

Vickie, "No one likes an extra wheel."

Cindy, "No, we talked about it, it would be fun."

Lana, "Come with us, Vickie."

Vickie looks at both of them and shakes her head no.

Cindy, "Vickie?"

Lana, "Forget it, Cindy, she is not going to go. She has a problem with me or maybe she just has a problem with lesbians."

Vickie, "I have no problem with lesbians."

Lana, "Then it is me."

Vickie, "It can be."

Lana now has Vickie's full attention, and Vickie has identified something that bothers her. So she begins to aggravate Lana to induce her into a fight. Vickie believes she is an abuser as well as a cheater and plays on acting rudely to bring out Lana's perceived character flaw.

Cindy, "Please guys stop. Just want us all to be friends."

Lana, "Don't think Vickie is going to let that happen. She sniffs something she doesn't like."

Vickie just smirks at Lana.

Lana, "You sniff something, Vickie, don't you, just like a dog?"

Vickie puts down her sandwich and asks, "Lana, I am curious about something since you brought up pets. Do you get furballs like cats do?"

Lana's face turns red as Cindy's mouth drops panning back and forth between, looking at both Vickie and Lana.

Vickie, "What's the matter, cat got your tongue?" Vickie takes a bite of her sandwich smiling at Lana as she chews. Lana has a mind to say many things and even take action but does not because she is caught between anger and attraction for Vickie. What Lana does not know is Vickie is well aware of this and playing on it.

Vickie, "Cindy, I guess if she coughs up a different color one then you know she is not faithful."

Lana stands up quickly staring knives at Vickie. "Let's go, Cynthia!"

Cindy slowly stands up as Vickie responds, "Cynthia huh? That is a very man thing to say."

Lana has a face of fury as she starts to walk off but stops and says, "Coming?"

Cindy gets up and leaves with a sorry look on her face to Vickie.

Vickie, "You guys have a great time at the movie."

Lana and Cindy walk off with Cindy looking back once in a while.

Later that night while Vickie reads a book, Cindy comes in and slams the door.

Cindy, "What the hell was that?"

Vickie pays no attention as she turns a page in the book.

Cindy, "I am talking to you, Vickie! What the hell was that? Are you trying to make enemies with Lana? She is the first real girlfriend I have had and you obviously have a problem with that."

Vickie, "I thought I was your girlfriend."

Cindy drops down on her bed. "You are, I mean Lana is my lover girlfriend."

"I know what you mean."

"Then what is going on?"

Vickie puts the book down. "You want to know?"

"God yes."

"As I have no issue with you having a lover girl, that girl is not good for you."

"Why?"

"She does not see you the way you see her."

"Oh really and how is that?"

Vickie looks at Cindy for a while. "Never mind, you will discover it for yourself."

"No, I want to know why."

"If I tell you, you will despise what I say. If you believe it, you will always wonder if I was wrong. You will find out for yourself, just be careful."

"Careful, am I an infant? I have had my heart broken before."

"Not what I am talking about."

"Oh so she is an abuser. Not everyone abuses people just because you grew up with that."

"I am just concerned for you, okay?"

"I'm sorry but my parents never beat the hell out of each other, so I don't think of people that way."

Vickie stands up and throws the book on her bed as she looks at Cindy. Vickie starts to leave as Cindy says, "I'm sorry, Vickie, I did not mean it."

Vickie leaves as Cindy holds her head in her hands. "Dummy."

Vickie walks around in the cool night. She wonders slowly thinking about the evening's conversation and eventually she stops. Vickie, "You can come out now." Vickie turns around and Lana walks out from the shadows.

Lana, "How did you know?"

"What are you doing here?"

Lana walks up to Vickie, "I don't want to be your enemy but a friend." Lana gets very close to Vickie's face and whispers, "Won't you be my friend?"

"What about Cynthia?"

"She is okay for now, but I think I need a real woman." Lana moves in slowly to kiss Vickie as Vickie leans back. Lana, "What is the matter? Scared of womanly companionship. You would think with all the bad men have done to you, you would want a woman."

"I see, Cindy has been talking to you."

"She likes to share, like most women. I want to share myself with you."

"You are a pretty girl, Lana, Cindy really loves you. Don't you respect her?"

Lana turns. "I need something more, Cindy is fun but I need someone who can physically keep up with me."

"Well then leave Cindy and keep looking."

"You going to tell Cindy, I suppose."

"No, she will figure you out soon enough. However, I do warn you, that you better be good to her. If you hurt her physically, you will get my attention."

Lana walks back over close to Vickie. "Really? And what would you do, Vickie?"

"I can hurt you in ways that you wish you did not know about."

"Oooh, I see. Well then, I guess that is that."

Lana begins to walk back to the dorm. "See you around."

Vickie stares at Lana leaving, the wheels begin to turn in Vickie's head.

Vickie walks back into the dorm as she passes the first floor and Lana's room. Lana stands in the doorway wearing a gray skimpy top and panties for Vickie to witness. Vickie walks by, "frigid." Lana slams the door. Vickie walks into her room and sits on the bed looking at Cindy who has her back turned and tucked away like she is sleeping. Vickie goes to the bathroom and gets ready for bed. As she returns, it is an eerie quiet, not even the usual sounds of people laughing from the dorm rooms.

Cindy, "Vickie."

Vickie, "Yes, Cin."

"I'm sorry for bringing up your parents."

"That is all right."

"Thank you. I love you, Vickie, good night."

"I love you too, Cin, sleep well."

Several weeks pass as Vickie and Lana very conspicuously ignore each other. Another evening and Cindy comes in from her visit with Lana.

Vickie, "Well, you are late tonight."

Cindy, "Yea, Lana's roomy left to go somewhere for a few days so we had the room to ourselves."

"Sounds hot."

"You may not like her but I tell you the sex is incredible."

Vickie responds, "Ah too much information."

"Sorry, it has just been awesome."

"That is good."

The next evening, Vickie comes back from martial arts class and Cindy is sitting in a fetal position crying. Vickie sits on the bed next to her. "What happened?" Cindy shakes her head no and buries herself in the pillow further. Vickie pulls Cindy's hair out her face and asks, "Cindy, what happened?"

Cindy with a cracking voice says, "Lana and I are over."

"I'm sorry."

Vickie grabs a tissue and says, "Sit up, let me wipe the tears."

Cindy sits up with her head down as Vickie lifts her head and sees a large bruise on her face. Vickie becomes infuriated. "Did Lana do this to you?"

Cindy cries and shakes her head yes.

Vickie wipes Cindy's face gently. "She got you good."

"It was my fault."

"What?"

"No, we had an argument because I caught another girl leaving her dorm room. She was not expecting me, and it was obvious they had just finished having sex. I exploded and called her a slut. She told me I was just a little girl and asked if I was going to sick you on her. I slapped her and she punched me in the face. I crawled out there as she kicked me in the butt, yelling at me."

"You know how to pick them."

"Please don't hurt Lana. I should have listened to you long ago."

"It is over and it is best to let it go now. But if she bothers you anymore you need to tell me."

"I will."

"Let me get something to fix you up." Vickie runs down to the store and gets some gauze and skin ointments. As she passes Lana's room the door opens.

Lana, "Vickie, I didn't mean it."

Vickie stops and turns around. "You're lucky this time."

"Tell Cindy I'm sorry. It just got out of control."

Vickie walks up to Lana as Lana is visibly becoming nervous. "Let me tell you something. Just because you want to be a man, does not mean you have to act like one. You hit another person, and I hit you but multiplied. Do we understand each other?" Lana motions her head yes. Vickie turns around and heads back to her room. As she arrives, Cindy is more composed as Vickie starts to treat her wound.

Cindy, "Why are you so good to me?"

Vickie, "Because you choose to be my friend and live with me despite the fact that trouble follows me and spills over to everyone around me."

"That is not true."

"Yea, how many times did you get attacked before you met me?"

"Well, none but that does not mean anything."

"Yes it does. Some people are made to have conflict in life."

"Well, I would rather deal with the conflict than not know you."

Vickie smiles. "Shut up and let me help you." Vickie bandages Cindy up and puts her to bed to which she dozes off quickly. Vickie plays with Cindy's hair and thinks that she wished this trouble had not reached Cindy. Vickie prepares to sleep.

A week later, Cindy arrives at lunch to sit next to Vickie.

Cindy, "It is starting to get really chilly."

Vickie, "I know, season is changing."

"Guess what?"

"What's that?"

"Lana got kicked out."

"Oh yea, what for?"

"Fighting with that girl I caught her with. Apparently something happened and they got into it. Campus police broke them up in the parking lot and Lana was kicked out."

"Yippee."

"C'mon, Vickie, that has to cheer you up some."

"I really don't care about Lana."

"Okay, well her roommate and I talked about Lana. She was terrified of her it seems. Lisa Wong is her name, she is nice."

"Hey maybe you two have something common."

Cindy raises her eyebrow and shrugs her shoulders as she takes a bite to eat.

A couple of nights later, Vickie notices that Cindy has not come in yet and it is unusually late for her. Vickie, concerned, goes out to look for her. Vickie wanders around in the dark and eventually sees two girls walking toward the dorm in the distance. Vickie hides behind a tree and watches. It is Cindy and Lisa, Lana's old roommate, and they are laughing, holding hands. They pass close enough that Vickie can hear Cindy say, "I had a wonderful time tonight, Lisa."

Lisa responds, "I wish I had met you last year."

They continue saying sweet things to each other as the voices fade from distance. Vickie smiles and waits for them to gain distance to not alert them she is following. They disappear into the building, and Vickie begins to move until a light catches her eye. Off in the distance of the dark moonless sky there is a blue-green light flickering too big to be a star. She watches as it slowly moves back and forth changing colors from blue to green. Then suddenly it vanishes. Vickie looks around in confusion as to what that was. She slowly walks to the dorm, ever watching for the lights to return but they do not. She goes into the dorm and sees Lisa's dorm room door cracked open and can hear Lisa and Cindy making out. She quietly moves by the door not to be noticed and makes her way to the room where she gets herself adjusted as if in bed. Minutes later, Cindy walks in quietly and sits down on the bed.

Vickie, "Where have you been?"

Cindy, "Out with Lisa."

"Had a good time?"

"You know, yea. She is very nice."

"That is good, well, good night."

"Good night, Vick."

Cindy goes to the bathroom to get ready for bed and quietly hums a tune. Vickie smiles and rolls over to sleep.

Observer

WHILE CINDY IS enjoying her new love, Vickie has been preoccupied with her business groups. However, one day she wanders across campus and visits the astronomy professor while he is in between classes. Vickie walks in the room as Professor Jack Chan welcomes her, "Hello there."

Vickie, "Hi, Mr. Chan, I am Vickie."

Jack, "Hi, Vickie, wait are you the Vickie who is…"

Vickie interrupts, "Afraid so."

"Well, I am honored, what can I do for you today?"

"I am just touring." Vickie walks by a telescope as Jack asks, "Astronomy interests you?"

"It used to."

"Well, you should take some courses."

"No, my interests are purely amateur."

Jack laughs. "So are most who come through this class. You used to like astronomy but no more?"

"When I was a kid I loved it. Dreamed of being an astronomer."

"Well, you can still enjoy it as a passion."

Vickie turns to the professor and smiles. "Yea, sure. I have taken too much of your time."

"You know what, how about you come by here at 10:00 p.m. tonight."

"I have a class that gets out about that time."

"No problem, come when you can. I have something I want to show you."

"What is it?"

"A telescope."

Vickie gives a partial smile. "Okay, I will be here."

"Great. See you then."

Vickie waves and leaves the room. After her martial arts class, she leaves straight to the astronomy room anxious to see what the professor has. She arrives and the professor greets her, "Vickie, welcome. Follow me."

Vickie follows him through a door at the front of the class. They go down a small hallway to a spiral staircase. Jack reaches the top and unlocks the door to the roof. They then turn around and there is a small observatory. Jack unlocks the two front doors and slides them open revealing a large telescope.

"Wow, I never knew this was here."

"It has been here for years. We built it in the middle of the roof to avoid as much light pollution as possible. It is not a great spot but then again this is not a great scope. But you can see much with it."

"This is a Newtonian, right?"

"That is right, you do have an interest."

"Well, I used to read about them all the time."

Jack enters the observatory and motions for Vickie to follow. Jack turns a computer on and selects an object. The observatory begins to move toward the object and the telescope beams in. Jack peers through the eyepiece adjusting and fine-tuning.

Jack, "Look through that."

Vickie approaches with a grin on her face and looks through the eyepiece. She sees the faint round shape with faint circles around it as she exclaims, "Saturn?"

"That's right."

Vickie looks again and Jack says, "Pick an object."

Vickie thinks, "Betelgeuse."

"Ah Orion." He dials in the star as the telescope moves toward it. He adjusts the viewer and Vickie looks.

Jack says, "It is not a very big scope so things are not that clear. But isn't this fun?"

"It's wonderful. I wish we had a comet to see."

"Sorry afraid no comets. But the great thing about space is that things are so far apart, even though they move very fast, you have plenty of time to watch them."

"Even meteors."

Jack laughs. "A little hard to see than a comet since there is no tail but technically sometimes."

"It is important to be able to track meteors. You know that is what killed the dinosaurs eventually."

"Yes it did but you can't catch them all."

They observed a few more galactic objects.

Vickie, "Well, thank you for showing me this. I have taken up your time too much."

"Nonsense, I practically live in this observatory. Any time the weather is good and you want to star watch with me, feel free."

"I will and thank you again. This meant a lot to me."

"No problem. One observer can always tell another."

Vickie is about to leave but she stops and asks, "Was there some star not too long ago that glowed bluish-greenish?"

Jack thinks, "No, there was not that I know of. Did you see one?"

"Yea, just for a short bit."

"Maybe you saw a UFO."

"Ah, I don't know about that."

"Well, I have not personally seen one but I tell you, keep your mind open. You never know."

Vickie laughs. "Okay, well, have a good night."

"Good night."

Vickie leaves as the professor engulfs himself in staring through his telescope.

The days seem to be stable and predictable as Vickie arrives in her room to see Lisa sitting there.

Vickie, "Hi, Lisa, waiting for Cindy?"

Lisa, "Actually waiting for you."

Vickie sits down. "Okay, I'm here."

"Cindy and I have been talking for a while now, and she could not bring herself to talk to you."

Vickie stands up and looks a Cindy's stuff. "She wants to move in with you."

Lisa takes a deep breath. "Yes. I'm sorry."

Vickie sits down next to Lisa, and she smiles at Lisa. "I'm happy for both of you."

"Really? You're not upset?"

"Not at all, I will help move her."

"Let me go and tell her. Thanks, Vickie."

Vickie stands up and smiles as Lisa leaves. The smile leaves Vickie's face as she sits on her own bed and then lays down to stare at the ceiling. A few minutes later, Lisa bursts in the room with some boxes and Cindy slowly walks in. "Hey, Vic."

Vickie stands up. "Hey, Cin, let me help you."

Cindy, "Thank you."

Lisa, "Hey, you have a lot of crap here, Cindy."

Cindy smiles at Vickie as Vickie returns the smile. "I know, I am a hoarder."

They all begin the process of carrying items down to Lisa's dorm room, and they have the final two small boxes as Lisa leaves to her room. Cindy stops and puts the box down near the door as Vickie stares on. Cindy runs over and hugs Vickie crying. "I love you, Vickie."

Vickie, "You are just going two stories down."

Cindy, "Silly, you know what I mean."

Vickie, "I know, I love you too."

Cindy stands in front of Vickie with a smile shadowed by sadness and tears on her face. Vickie wipes the tears from Cindy's face and gives her a kiss. Cindy holds her hand over her mouth as if a waterfall is being held back of tears. Vickie smiles. "See you around, Cin."

Cindy smiles, crying, and shaking her head yes, choked up. Cindy grabs her box and takes one last look at Vickie. As Vickie walks over to the door and watches Cindy walking down the hallway, she closes the door.

It is late at night and Vickie can't sleep staring at Cindy's side of the room. Vickie gets dressed and wanders out. She makes it to the main campus building and looks to the top. Chan is looking through his telescope as usual, and Vickie walks up to the observatory.

Chan, "Aw, Ms. Newsome, good to see you again. Up late tonight?"

Vickie, "Couldn't sleep, thought I would check on you."

Chan motions her to enter the observatory as she does and sits down in an extra chair. "What is keeping you so late, UFOs?"

Vickie, "No, my roommate moved out."

"I think that happens a lot."

"It does but she was here with me from year one. She met a nice girl and they are serious about each other."

"Oh I see. I guess it is lonely in there now."

"Yea, I miss her whiney talks. You really don't get lonely out here?"

"Naw, I have myself to keep me company. What better company could I ask for?"

Vickie laughs. "I guess so. What are you looking at tonight?"

"Looking at one of the stars of Pleiades."

"Aw the seven sisters."

"That's right. You know there are cultures that believe we came from there."

"Well, that is ridiculous. The stars are not even close to each other, they just look close from our vantage point. How could anything reach here from there?"

Chan laughs. "You would make a good astronomer. That is correct. But it is not ridiculous. People need myths."

"Lies are important."

Chan looks at her. "Yes they are. You see, myths keep us moving forward. Belief is a powerful creative force. Belief becomes perception and that becomes reality."

"How can what someone merely believes become reality. I mean I know that works in business but in nature?"

"Especially in nature. You see, there is an experiment in which light is divided into two. Same light, same source, but one of those lights are observed and the other not. They can actually measure a change in the two lights."

Vickie looks confused. "How?"

"Because observation can change things. It is actually a principal in physics."

Vickie laughs. "I'm sorry but you have lost me."

"What happens when you see something? What takes place in your head?"

"The light is received by my eyes and is transmitted as electrical signal to my brain."

"Correct, your brain interprets electrical signals and makes a visual picture it thinks it saw from your eyes. Your mind thinks it is seeing everything as the eyes see it but it is only perception; perception which your mind interprets as reality. Energy is used to give you a perception. Your mind invents the reality of it. Somehow in physics, the interpretation of visual signals your eyes receive and the way your brain perceives it affects what you are observing. On some subatomic level, your mind is changing what you are focused on."

"Are you a scientist or science-fiction writer?"

"You can talk to anyone in quantum physics, you will find what I am telling you is true."

"So in some way our brain is able to influence energy of light."

"Everything, matter, all of it. That is why it is important for you to believe things. That is why myths are important.

They not only keep people moving to a goal, it creates the path to that goal."

"Okay. I get it."

"No you don't. You see the entire universe has structure, method, and organization. To us, it seems like chaos but it really is not. Sure, things move, collide, and after the big bang, spread apart. But it is obvious to me that someone observed everything and it moves based on their observation."

Vickie looks with a confused look and then realizes. "God, you are talking about God."

"That's right. God, some kind of energy neuro-network that has consciousness, whatever you call it, it exists. It thinks and observes. It influences everything."

"You are saying the universe is a living thing? Energy somehow became a thinking brain?"

"Hard to imagine, you have the same thing in a microform. It could happen in a macroform too, energy is energy. You use energy to think, maybe he does too."

"That is just too weird for me."

"You see, whatever you think is out there is only important if it helps you."

"Maybe it observed you and that observation changed you to understand something is out there."

Chan smiles and leans back. "Now you are thinking."

"I don't pretend to understand mythological concepts, but I will have to take your word for it."

"Don't take my word for it, just observe things and derive your own theories. When you find a theory that works for you, believe in it. In the end, that is all we really have. Beliefs. What do we really know?"

Vickie stands. "Well, that is a lot to think about. I think I am ready for bed now."

Chan laughs. "Better than a sleeping pill, right?"

"No, you are not boring. It really helped me to sit here and listen to your observations."

"You see, observations do change things."

Vickie smiles. "Indeed they do. Good night, wizard."

"Good night, Valkyrie."

Vickie turns around from leaving. "Excuse me?"

"You are a Valkyrie. Mythological woman who takes the worthy people to Valhalla. That is what I observe about you."

"If only I knew were Valhalla is."

"It is anywhere you take them. A good person will take them where they belong."

Vickie turns around and leaves confused as once in a while she looks back, and Chan is staring at her. She leaves to her dorm room and stares at the ceiling from her bed. She drifts off to sleep as she tries to process a very confusing talk with Professor Chan.

Graduation

THE DAY ARRIVES and Vickie has achieved her bachelor of business management and has put herself on the path to work on her masters but she wants to proceed to the work world. She stands in line to receive her diploma and notices that Chip Sanders and Doctor Smith are in the audience amid the excited hopeful parents all snapping pictures and smiling. Doctor Smith nods his head and Chip gives a thumbs-up. Vickie smiles back feeling good that someone was there to watch her graduation. The students sit down in front as the ceremony calls for the graduates with honors. Names are called and the dean calls out the summa cum laude and the magna cum laude recipients as everyone applauds and they make short speeches. Then the dean says, "In the history of this university, this has never happened before. We have never given this honor before because it has never seen such a student before. We have been blessed with many great students but this one's efforts and achievements have not gone unnoticed. Vickie Newsome, please come up." Vickie rises and is astonished she is called. She walks up to the dean and stands in attention.

Dean says, "Vickie Newsome, this university bestows upon you the first time honor of maxima cum laude." The dean places the medal and ribbon around her neck as the students erupt in a standing ovation. Whistles and yells of Vickie's name burst from the graduates. Vickie is motioned to make a speech as the dean sits down. Vickie, "Wow, I did not expect this. I really don't know what to say but thank you. I guess the thing that I can say is to never stop no matter what is against you. No matter how hot the fires in life get, they just temper you as one great man said to me. A great man that is sitting out there tonight. Another one sitting out there showed that there is no shame in sharing one's self. If you truly are strong you can allow yourself to be vulnerable. I am strong enough. I can shoulder the troubles I have and the troubles of others. I only leave those in my life's wake that cause these troubles. Those who are deserving are welcome in the journey. I am thankful and grateful for my life. May we all find peace and happiness in whatever we go out and do. This is for you, Mom, I love you. Thank you!"

Everyone stands and applauds as Vickie steps off the stage back to her seat. The dean gets up and says, "Our commencement speaker today is Senator Ken Wright who is an alumni here back in the day. Matter of fact, he and I were in the same fraternity and shared a room. It is my honor to present my friend and the honorable Senator Wright. Senator Wright stands up and shakes the dean's hand.

Ken, "Thank you, Tom, for that warm welcome. Being here and seeing my old friend sure brings back a lot of memories. Congratulations to all you graduates and honor winners. Vickie, I was moved by your speech, well done." Vickie listens intently as the senator talks about careers and times and how politics have shaped him. He gives lofty assessments and quotes from other great politicians. Vickie is enamored with his speech despite the fact she knows it was probably wrote by a professional speech writer. However, she likes it all the same. After the speech and ceremony has ended, everyone is hugging and congratulating each other. Cindy and Lisa come up to Vickie.

Cindy, "Oh my God, I am stunned by the honor you got."

Vickie, "No one more stunned than me."

Lisa, "Congrats, Vickie."

Vickie, "Thank you, Lisa. So where to guys from here?"

Cindy, "My parents' company. Lisa is going to work with me."

Vickie, "What does your dad say?"

Cindy, "He is fine with it. We are going to live with them for a bit till we get our own place."

Cindy and Lisa hold each other smiling.

Vickie, "I wish the best for the both of you."

Cindy, "What about you? You know, I could still talk to my parents about giving you a position there, at least temporarily."

Vickie, "I appreciate it but I have a choice of internships available to me and I plan to get my masters."

Cindy walks over and gives Vickie a hug crying. She gives Vickie a kiss on the cheek and cups her cheek with her hand.

Cindy, "I love you, Vickie, and you take care of yourself."

Cindy and Lisa wave good-bye as they go back to waiting Cindy's parents. Vickie waves at Cindy's parents and they wave back. Then Doctor Smith walks over and shakes Vickie's hand.

Smith, "Congratulations, Vickie. Not sure the world is ready for you."

Vickie, "Thank you for helping me back in high school."

"I am not so sure I did anything that you already were not working out."

"I was on the edge and you pushed me back over to stable ground."

"Yea, but in just a few days you seem to be together."

"Intellectually yes and I knew what I needed to do but was still depressed. It eventually passed."

"It usually does. Well, I need to get back. I just wanted to see your graduation."

"I am glad you came, not sure how you heard about it."

"Word got around. More people know about you than you think."

Smith smiles and walks on his way. Chip makes his way over, and Vickie gives him a hug.

Chip, "I have never heard of the honor they gave you, wow."

Vickie, "Me neither, I don't know what to say."

"You earned it. You paid your dues and now ready to take on the world."

"Thank you for being here and for helping my last year in high school."

"You are welcome. Say, where are you going from here anyway?"

"I will be here doing a business internship at a local company while I finish with my masters. I want to complete my teaching credential too. Maybe sometime I will teach some high schoolers. But I have some things to finish up here with my martial arts classes, so forth."

"That martial arts stuff is pretty important to you, isn't it?"

"It is more than martial arts, it is strategy and understanding motion and flowing with that motion. It is hard to explain but it works in everything."

"Well, I am astonished how much you have grown in these past five years. You are now an incredible lady. I am proud of you. Like you were my own daughter."

"That is sweet of you."

"I never told you that I had a daughter."

"I knew you were divorced, but no I did not know you had children."

"We had a daughter but she died at age four from leukemia. We never got over it and divorced. It took a lot of years for me to put myself together. Then I woke up to some things and got my life back. That is why I like being a motivational speaker. But when I saw you broken up, I saw my daughter. Silly I know but in a way helping you was like getting to experience having a daughter who grew up."

"Not silly at all." She hugs him for a long time. "Thank you for being a dad to me."

Chip gets choked up. "You are welcome. Well, I better go."

"Yea, I have some people to go see too."

"Keep in touch."

They hug as Vickie says, "I will."

Everyone begins to disband as a few students visit with Vickie as she makes her way through.

Vickie has found her a small apartment nearby that is just a bus ride to possible intern jobs she is thinking about and close to the school and martial arts gym so she can finish her masters and martial arts training. It is a quaint-efficiency apartment on the third floor with a little balcony that looks straight at the university in the distance. A mere bicycle ride over. She can even see the observatory on the campus building which helps to think at night. Spending her summer in solitude focusing on her projects, she spends no time dating. The offers pour in from companies for positions having heard of her honors. She has some money and has invested part to grow. She spends little and saves much. She finds herself spending more and more time at the local bookstore finding new adventures to read about. She is not much on science fiction or romance novels but particularly likes nonfiction stories of struggle and triumph. She reads them almost like religious tracts, studying them and figuring out the dynamics of each person's situation. This is her life for part of the summer. She eventually settles on a job that intrigues her and the interview goes well. She is hired and on Monday she starts. She goes shopping for business-appropriate dresses to carry her for a while. She is set and ready to go. Ready to start her adventure in life, with only the rest of the week and the weekend to relax before it all starts.

First Day

Vickie arrives for her first day of work at a new job at King's Way Marketing. CEO Stan King is a colorful man who has been on the news a time or two for his eccentric promotions. He caters not to big companies but mid to small companies that don't mind a little embarrassment in advertisement. King has plenty of embarrassments to share. She had summer interned before for a week at a time for others but for some reason this company caught her eye. As she approaches the security desk she is sent up to the fifth floor where she is to meet the director of marketing John Taylor for this small but seemingly successful company.

John, "Are you Ms. Newsome?"

Vickie, "Please, Vickie and yes I am."

"Vickie, welcome to King's Way where we do things… King's way. John King's way that is, I am John Taylor, the director here. I, more or less, implement what is decided here. Let me show you around. Oh and please call me John. Mr. Taylor thing makes me feel old.”

Vickie smiles as John shows her bathrooms to break rooms and tells her briefly the most important policies out of the hundreds she and no one else will ever remember in the employee handbook. He introduces her to various people working there until they arrive at Stan King's door.

John, “This is Mr. King's office, before we go in, I have to warn you he is kind of unpredictable and a little, well, rude.”

Vickie, “No problem, Mr. Taylor.”

John takes a breath and knocks on the door. A deep bellow rings out, “Come on in!”

John and Vickie walk in the large office that has Stan's desk to one side near a corner and a small conference table on the other side of the room. Vickie pans around the room quickly as she sees plaques with golf hole-in-one awards, mounted deer heads as well as pictures of Stan and buddies from days long past. Stan gets up and walks over as John says, “Mr. King, this is Vickie Newsome our new marketing research intern.”

Stan approaches extending his hand and Vickie smiles shaking his hand. “Nice to meet you, sir.”

Stan, “Sir? We need to work on that and a strong handshake. Feels like I just shook hands with a pro boxer.”

Vickie, "Well, I work out and like to beat up boxers."

Stan and John look at each other as Stan says. "Well, all right then." Stan laughs and asks, "Vickie, I'm sorry can I call you that?"

Vickie barely nods yes as he continues, "Well, we here at King's Way like to advertise out of the box so to speak. We offer everything from straightforward marketing campaigns to shock ones. We are not afraid here to do what it takes to generate human emotion to think about our client's products." Stan walks over to his awards and very obviously draws attention to them and his hunting trophies as he gives his King's speech. After he stops standing under a large buck deer, he asks, "Have any questions, dear?"

Vickie, "Just one, dear, about your deer."

Stan smiles and stands straight proud of his kill.

Vickie, "Did you kill that deer?"

Stan looks up at it. "Why yes I did."

"Did you stalk it or did you sit in a tree house and shoot it? You know, while it ate corn from your automated feeder."

John looks down at the ground as if there is something on the carpet needing his attention. Stan stares at Vickie as she has a half grin on her face.

Stan, "Why, Vickie, I shot this animal as it was standing on a small peak. I had been tracking it all day and it took several shots to bring it down. I had to get several people to come help me bring it back, it was so large."

Vickie, "Well then it was a nice kill."

Stan, "Yes, it was. Anyway, welcome aboard and I look forward to your contributions to my company."

Vickie, "Thank you, sir, for the opportunity."

John and Vickie leave Stan's office. John tells Vickie quietly, "Mr. King shot the deer in the butt and it took his guide to kill it. He walked back while they drag the thing back to the camp."

Vickie laughs. "To be expected."

John walks Vickie to a small office next to his. "We have plenty of space here. This is yours. Your primary job here will be to assist me and God knows I need it."

Vickie, "Overwork you they do?"

John, "Well, the way it works is that we, as a group, will throw out ideas and Mr. King will yea or nay them and then expound on the one he likes. It then comes from his brain to us for action. We create an action plan based on his thinking and then it is my job to carry it out."

Vickie, "So basically a team of people design a marketing campaign on the way that they think Stan would want it. Then he takes one of those ideas he can easily mold into his own and changes it totally. The team takes his idea and then creates a to-do list for you to carry it out. Right?"

"Pretty much that and it is Mr. King, not Stan. Any questions?"

"How many interns have you gone through?"

"Seven."

"Outstanding."

John shows Vickie where the office supply cabinet is as Vickie prepares her desk. A little later, John asks her to come in his office.

"Okay, Vickie, here is a list of the action items yet to be done on this one campaign."

Vickie looks at the paper, and it is a campaign for a small beer distributer. She intently looks at the company being represented and just blanks for a moment. John looks at the paper and back at Vickie. "Is there a problem?"

Vickie breaks from the gaze. "No, not at all." She smiles and says, "I will work on the next action item for you now."

"That would be greatly appreciated."

She leaves as John runs his fingers through his hair and takes a deep breath.

Wednesday afternoon arrives and Vickie walks into John's office.

Vickie, "John, here is the paperwork for the action items."

John looks at the stack and says, "Done already on that action item."

"No, all them, there were only three left."

"I know but give yourself some slack. We have weeks to get this done."

John thumbs through it as Vickie sits down in front of his desk. After about ten minutes. "Okay, Vickie, it looks good. Let me comb through it more specifically and check it all. Good work."

Vickie smiles and returns to her office. John thinks, *Lord, she will have my job soon.*

Vickie stares out the office window at the street below and thinks, *I like this.*

John walks in with the files to her office and says, "They're good, we have one little issue. Mr. King likes to have them formatted a certain way. We have a template on the server. If you can just format it to that template and reprint them, it would work. And take your time, no rush."

"No problem." Vickie looks at the files and realizes that she may be too enthusiastic. So she finds the template and copies the data to the correct format. It only takes her the rest of the day but she acts like it took her all week. The next Monday morning, Vickie is looking up things on the Internet to waste time as usual.

John comes in. "Vickie, are you done making the documents in the right template?"

Vickie, "They are right here, let me bring them to you."

John returns to his office as Vickie brings them in. John. "Thanks, Vickie."

"John, is it always going to be like this?"

"Vickie, one thing you learn is if you do things too fast then it becomes expected. Then someday you mess up or don't do it as fast and you are replaced. Understand?"

"I understand."

John checks the files and takes them to the staff meeting to update Stan and others where they are at.

John returns and says to Vickie. "Hey, Vickie, Mr. King would like to see you in his office."

"What for?"

"Not sure but be polite and remember Mr. King."

Vickie leaves to Stan's office and knocks on the door.

"Come in!" bellows from Stan. "Vickie, come in and have a seat."

Vickie sits down facing Stan as he plays with his mustache rocking back and forth. He has a smug look on his face as he stares at Vickie. He is wearing his two-tone dress shirt that looks half blue-collar work shirt and have professional executive and khaki pants to appear hunter like. He fancies himself to look like Teddy Roosevelt with his dirty blond hair and freckles. Aftershave and cologne battle for dominance giving the aroma of a turpentine truck that has crashed into a cigar shop. The office is silent with only the sound of a digital clock acting like a mechanical timepiece. He enjoys the uneasy silence knowing that his employee is held hostage ten feet away from him with forty yards of office behind them.

Stan, "You are doing a great job so far, I just wanted you to know that."

Vickie, "Thank you, sir."

"John tells me you diligently got those last three action items taken care of and reported in just one week. That is fantastic. I know that is probably new-person enthusiasm, but good all the same."

Vickie stares and says, "Just want to get it done."

"Tell me, could you have done them in two days?"

"No, I am not sure what to do. You know, my first assignment."

"Yea, but you interned before and learned this stuff in college. This is normal procedural stuff."

Vickie just stares.

"What I am confused about is the server shows you edited these documents without the templates by Wednesday and then had them redone on templates by the end of the day. John did not bring them into us for an update till today. So what happened between the rest of last week?"

"I had to thoroughly check everything and that took a while."

Stan smiles and sits forward putting his hands together and elbows on his desk. "Hell. You had them done in no time at all and John told you to slow down. How do I know? It is obvious by the server dates on the files and he has done it with other interns."

Vickie has an upset look on his face.

Stan, "Let me let you in on a little secret. John is on his way out. I am looking to replace him. That is why we have interns to work for him. Learn the ropes and then replace him. However, he manages to run them off after a while."

"Why don't you just fire him?"

"I would but I need him until someone can fill his shoes. Are you that person?"

"And If I do? How long till you are asking my intern the same thing?"

Stan leans back and laughs a little. He starts laughing more and stands up walking to the window. He looks at Vickie and shakes his finger at her. "You have a little personality to you, I like that."

Vickie stands up and walks over to Stan and stares in his eyes. "I doubt that."

"Listen here, young lady, there are limits to what I allow my people to talk to me like."

"I have heard and it seems to shrink as time goes on."

Stan looks upset and then calms and laughs. "You are funny, I like that." Stan puts his hands on Vickie's shoulders and says, "You are going to be just what we need around here." He puts his hands to his side, as Vickie puts her hand on his shoulder and says, "You know something, Stan, you are just a little boy who likes bullying people around. I can't stand you or the way you smell. So good-bye, I think I need to find somewhere else to work than a low-rent marketing company that caters to the bottom of the barrel industries."

Stan's face turns red as he is about to erupt and Vickie makes her way to the door and opens it. "By the way, Stan, next time you go hunting just let the guides shoot it for you." Vickie slams the door behind her as she gets her personal things from her office.

John steps in. "What happened?"

Vickie looks at John. "He was too critical of my work and said we needed a better intern."

John looks on as Vickie leaves.

JOB (Just Over Broke)

VICKIE CONTACTS THE next prospect of her list of job opportunities. This one is another small marketing firm but the CEO is a woman who has had write-ups about her skills in turning this once-failing company around. Vickie looks forward to the job as they have interviewed and offered her the opening position. She arrives on the first day as she is given an orientation by executive secretary Tina for the CEO Sandy Thompson.

Tina, "We have a cubicle for you right here. Ms. Thompson will be in this afternoon for the Monday's rally. Just follow all the other sales execs in the conference room when we call for it."

Vickie, "Excuse me, sales exec, I thought I was interning for a marketing position."

Tina, "You are, we call them sales execs around here." Tina gives her a big fake smile and scurries off to her desk to check her makeup in a little mirror.

Vickie pans around the other cubicles and room as she hears the constant chatter of other sales execs on the phones soliciting advertisement space for local TV and radio. It has become very apparent that she is just settled into an inside sales phone job. However, she reads the company policies and guide to the workplace book on her desk. The morning drones on as administrative people hand out sheets on each cubicle desk to each person. Vickie looks at the papers as they talk about new accounts sold as well as quotes from famous motivational speakers. Vickie says out loud to herself, "I just died and went to work hell." The person next to her is Jim and he overhears here saying, "Hell, oh no. That is later." He smiles and continues back on the phones. Tina comes by and tells Vickie, "Vickie, you will be trained on the phones today, and we will get you an assigned call list and dialogue sheet so you can start selling tomorrow."

Vickie, "Dialogue sheet?"

Tina, "Yes, it is a sheet with various ways to talk to customers to sell our ad time." Vickie half-smiles and nods yes as Tina gives a big smile and walks back to her desk.

Lunch time arrives and everyone, like a herd of buffalo, leave at the same time and head to break room or sandwich place in the building on the first floor. Vickie slowly takes her smoothie to the break room and sits down. Everyone is dissociative and focuses on eating their lunch constantly looking at the clock. Vickie just smiles back when one of them catches her looking. Five minutes till the lunch time is over and everyone cleans up and leaves back to their cube as efficient as any military-drilled soldier. Vickie slowly stands up and says, "Did I get hired or drafted?"

It is one o'clock and the IT person comes by to teach her how to log into her phone. IT tells her that they measure the amount of calls she makes, time spent, and call backs to same numbers. Every week they will post on the corkboard everyone's phone efficiency times. He advises to make sure you are not at the bottom.

Vickie, "Why, what happens if you are on the bottom?"

IT, "Just don't be there."

He leaves and Vickie stares at the phone. Two o'clock rolls around and the CEO Sandy has arrived. She is tall, strong looking, very confident, has dark long hair, and storms into her office straight away. The general volume of people talking on the phones increase as well as speed now. About thirty minutes later over the speaker, Tina announces three o'clock sales exec meeting. Vickie just watches the CEO pace and talk on the speakerphone until it is meeting time. About five minutes before the meeting, the salespeople cut their calls short and start shuffling to the conference room. Vickie follows behind them finding a seat in the back. The room is very quiet as everyone waits. Tina comes in with handouts passing to everyone. Vickie looks down and it is the latest call results of the sales execs for the previous week. A few minutes later, Sandy walks in saying, "Sorry, guys, had to fix an issue with one of our clients." She makes her way to front. "Okay. You all have your numbers, good effort last week. Only one person fell down on the job and that was you, Frank. Could you stand up and tell us what happened?"

An old heavyset Frank stands up and looks around as all the others stare at him like a leper. Frank, "Well, I had a run of customers that were just stonewalling me that whole week but today is much better."

Sandy, "Anyone else get stonewalled?"

Everyone sits like statues slightly shaking their heads no.

Sandy, "No one else had a problem, Frank. Go ahead and come sit in the chair of shame." Frank makes his way to the front and faces everyone. Sandy, "Why do we even need this chair? If everyone did their job consistently we could get rid of it. Anyway you have the numbers, let's see if we can get them a little better this week. Today, we have a new sales exec, Vickie, is it?"

Vickie stands up. "That is right."

Tina whispers a few things into Sandy's ear.

Sandy, "Vickie comes straight from the university and received high marks there. I am sure she is going to show some of you, old brooms, how a new broom can sweep like. Welcome aboard, Vickie."

Vickie, "Thank you, ma'am." Vickie sits down totally baffled by what she is witnessing.

Sandy, "Now several of you have been taking sick days lately. From my understanding it is summer and not flu season. I know this is a stressful job but you do get paid 2 percent commission on top of pay, so if you can't handle it, leave. There are plenty of people who would be proud to have an air-conditioned job with lots of income potential and all they have to do is talk on the phone. Damn, people, we are not 9-1-1 operators here, we are just selling ad space." Sandy walks around with an amazed look of disgust on her face. "I know you have heard it before, but this is for Vickie's benefit. I used to do what you are doing right now and holy shit was I good at it. I sold more than any other execs and you know why? Not because I am pretty, the customer can't see me on the phone. Not because I have the voice of a rock star, it is kind of grindy actually. It is because I am not a lazy piece of crap is why. I know this crap is not going to sell itself, I had to. I have a mind to jump on that phone and show you how it is done. I think you guys have what it takes to win big at this game but your heart for some reason is not always in it. Is it me? Am I so hard on you because I want you to win? Do you hate my guts because I am the boss and I would never date any of you losers in a million years? Well, I challenge you to take that hate and turn it into cash. Prove me wrong. Prove to me that you are a success."

Vickie is astonished and small flame of defiance begins to grow in her. Normally, she would just walk away from a nightmare like this but Vickie feels the need to stay. She watches as Sandy berates the personnel individually one after another looking at sales charts. Finally, at the end of the meeting, Sandy walks over to Frank and puts her hand on his shoulder.

Sandy, "Frank, you earned Goober this week."

Frank looks down wiping his head with his hand.

Sandy, "Johnson, you have Goober don't you, go get him out the pen."

Johnson steps out and in a few minutes walks in with a goat on a leash.

Vickie thinks, *What the hell?*

Johnson walks the goat and hands the leash to Sandy. Sandy grabs the leash and says, "When you fail, you have to take care of Goober for a week. Frank, the honor is all yours." She hands the leash to Frank as he looks up at Sandy.

Sandy smiles back. "Okay, guys, go get them."

Everyone shuffles out quick as Vickie sits and watches. Frank escorts the goat out and to a room it is kept in called the pen where it has water and food. But at night the unlucky sales exec has to take the goat home and keep it for a week unless their numbers are bad for another week. Usually most only have to keep it a week.

Vickie is about to leave when Sandy says, "Nice to meet you, Vickie, come to my office."

Vickie follows Sandy into her office and Sandy shuts the door. Vickie looks around and there are no chairs anywhere.

Sandy, "I would offer you a seat, but I don't like to sit down. I prefer to talk on speakerphone and pace. It helps me think. Good for fitness too. You look fit, you work out?"

Vickie, "I hold several black belts in the martial arts."

"Excellent. I took some myself at one time. I love running though. You had high marks from your college, very high. Solid group participation in college and you obviously are an achiever. You know, I have managers who manage the other departments but the sales one I personally control because it is the most critical. However, I am thinking that if I ever met the right woman, they could take that over for me."

Vickie, "Woman, you mean person?"

Sandy smiles. "Those guys need a woman to lead them. Look at them, they are mostly all men who miss their mothers. They need someone to parent them at all times; otherwise, they would not take this abuse. They need a strong woman to guide them; otherwise, men stray and get lazy from their tasks. You think you would like to be their guide someday?"

"I am not sure I could do it as well as you."

"Naw, you could learn. I tell you, if you get on those phones like I did long ago and prove yourself, you will be running this crew."

Vickie stares at Sandy but offers no body language. Sandy looks her up and down. "Well, that is my motivational speech for you. Any questions?"

"Just one. You really enjoy your job?"

Sandy smiles. "I love it."

Vickie nods her head yes and walks out the office. Vickie sits down at her cube and Jim, next to her, says, "Got to meet the boss, eh? What did she want?"

Vickie smiles and says, "She just wanted to welcome me aboard and offered that someday I could manage you guys."

Jim's smile turns to concern as he quickly gets back to the phone for the next call. Vickie grins to herself and says, "Oh boy."

The week goes on and Vickie has made calls and sold some ads but her phone performance has brought her to the bottom of the charts. By Monday afternoon, it is sales exec meeting time and Sandy walks in.

Sandy, "Well, crew, that is much better this last week. I am almost impressed. However, we have a new person at the bottom. Vickie, could you come up here and sit in the seat of shame."

Vickie gets up and proudly walks down to sit in the seat of shame.

Sandy, "I had high hopes for you, Vickie, so you better get it together. Frank, bring Vickie Goober please."

Frank jumps up and quickly retrieves the goat. He hands the leash to Vickie as Sandy says, "Okay, back to the phones you jerks." Sandy smiles at Vickie and Vickie smiles back.

Vickie takes the goat to the pen and gets back to the phones. At the end of the day, Vickie puts the goat in her new car and tries to keep it calm as possible. She sneaks it in and out her apartment each day.

Thursday comes and Vickie asks Tina, "Can I see Sandy for a moment."

Tina buzzes Sandy and Vickie is welcomed in.

Sandy, "What can I do for you, Vickie?"

Vickie, "I am sorry my sales were down, I am new and I know that is not an excuse. Can I show my enthusiasm by bringing up some lunch tomorrow for the guys?"

Sandy smiles. "Why that is a wonderful idea. Look forward to it."

"Hope you like potato salad?" Vickie leaves in good spirits.

The next day at lunch, everyone is called into the break room because Vickie has made them lunch. Everyone is enjoying a variety of vegetables and barbeque. Sandy has a barbeque sandwich and says, "Vickie, that is good, you grill this up?"

Vickie, "Yes I did, took all evening."

Everyone is chowing down as Sandy asks, "Interesting tasting. What type of barbeque is this?"

Vickie says, "Goober."

Room is dead silent as everyone stops eating and looks at their meat sandwiches. Vickie throws the goat leash on one of the tables as everyone looks at it.

Sandy, "Your joking, right?"

Vickie, "I never kid about goats. I know it gets your goat but I quit." Vickie leaves as the room as everyone looks at each other and Sandy stands like a statue. Vickie hums a tune and sings a bit about goats as she leaves with a smile.

Third Time is a Charm

Vickie takes a few days to rethink her first two jobs. She combs through the internship offers a little more critically as there is one she passed up because the company was a bit of a startup. She thinks that maybe there is a better opportunity there being a new company. The pay is not as good but it maybe an opportunity to affect the culture a little before it turns vampire weird like the first two. She goes to an interview with the CEO and founder of Dynamic Marketing, Tom Patterson. Vickie arrives in his office as they shake hands and sit.

Tom, "Vickie, I am quite surprised you are interested in here with your credentials from college."

Vickie, "Well, I tried out a couple of established companies already and it just did not seem to work out well."

"What happened?"

"The first one was a jungle and the second one was a goat."

Tom laughs a little. "Goat, okay. We are fairly laid back here. My personal view on employees is they are grown adults and I should not have to baby them. I have to support them and give them the tools they need but empower them to do what they know to do. I feel that if I help my people and put them first in turn they will do the same. If you treat employees badly they have no motivation and maybe even will do malicious compliance to sabotage you. I don't need that here. There is no reason work can't be something to look forward to and enjoy. Everyone is like family here. Sure, we have a black sheep in our family, but it keeps the mix interesting. How does that sound to you?"

"It sounds great. I think your philosophy is sound."

"What are you looking for in a career?"

"I like the idea of shaping people's thought process through marketing. I know we may do campaigns for things that are harmful like alcoholic beverages but I will perform my job as well as anything else."

"That is good to hear, but I do not work for anything alcohol related. There is good money in it and I have no issue with alcohol manufacturers but I am a recovering alcoholic, sober ten years now, and I simply do not want to work for them."

Vickie smiles. "My dad was an alcoholic and it killed him."

"I am sorry to hear that. I nearly drank myself to death too."

"He did not drink himself to death but it did do him in."

Tom looks for a bit. "If it gets away from you then unfortunately that is inevitable. Anyway, what is your ultimate goal if you worked for my company?"

"For it to be my company."

Tom smiles. "That may take a long time but anything can happen. Let me show you around the place."

They get up and Tom takes her on a tour of the twenty-person company. He then shows her a small-windowed office and says, "This would be your office if you accepted a position here."

Vickie, "Am I being offered a position here?"

"Vickie, I would be a fool to pass up on offering someone with your honors a job here. I can't pay the norm for starters unfortunately but maybe if we grow bigger, I can make some adjustments."

Vickie looks out the window and turns around. "I accept."

"Really? I mean, welcome aboard." They shake hands as Tom is excited. "Start anytime you like."

"How about Monday?"

"Monday it is. Let me get you to the HR person to get you situated away and then we will see you Monday."

Vickie and Tom go to the HR person as Vickie fills out paperwork and then leaves for home. She has a good feeling about the place even though it pays lower to start. But Vickie has plans to change all that.

Monday comes and Vickie walks in the door of her new job. Tom is there to greet her, "Vickie, welcome to your new job. I already got your office outfitted with a desk and stuff to get you going." He walks her over to her office and it looks nice. Brand-new furniture and even a tall plant in the corner. "What do you think?"

Vickie pans around. "Very nice, thank you, Mr. Patterson."

"Tom, I am Tom around here. I may be your boss but we are all partners in success here."

Vickie smiles. "Okay, Tom. What should I do first?"

"Well, why don't you get your office organized the way you want for a while. In a couple of hours, I will call a meeting and introduce you to the gang. After that, we will get with you one on one and show you what we need and give you some things to work on."

Vickie, "Sounds great."

Tom leaves as Vickie walks around her office, running her fingers down her new desk. She sits in the comfortable chair and spins around a couple of times stopping at the windows behind her. She stares at the six floors down, overlooking a park nearby. A feeling of warmth washes over her as she starts to organize things. Later, a meeting is called and Tom introduces Vickie to the team. They discuss the projects at hand and give Vickie a rundown of where they are at. She feels very welcomed as they talk to her as if she had been working there all along. She asks questions and her suggestions are addressed and respected. It is an environment of respect she has not seen in the first two jobs. After the meeting, she converses with some of the workers. The IT manager Mike Sims tells her that her notebook workstation just came in today and he will have it set up for her by the end of the day. She thanks him as Tom asks if she would come in his office to go into the business further. They spend time working on things and then Tom takes Vickie to lunch.

Vickie, "Thank you for lunch."

Tom, "You are welcome, I hope you like the food. I can eat their sandwiches every day it seems."

"They are good. Thank you for the opportunity at your company."

"Vickie, we don't get top-shelf college graduates come to work with us every day. My guys are great and talented in their own right, but we need more good people. I think we can land some bigger accounts and do very well against the big guys if we just have the right chemical mixture in our employee pool. I have a good feeling about you. You seem very confident and, despite your young age, very experienced."

"Well, I have been through a lot and that tends to mature you up quickly."

"Yea, I am sure."

"So how did you start this company?"

"I started it five years ago when I left a large marketing firm. I was a vice president there but things changed with them and the culture was not suited for my tastes anymore."

"They were cutting you out of things, right?"

"No, not really. I was in the inner circle, so to speak, but there is a degree of the way people can be treated that I did not like. It was not happening to me but others. I just felt I needed to change things. I took a chance, put all my eggs in one basket, and started Dynamic."

"Did your wife like that?"

Tom looks down at his ring and says, "No, not married anymore. She left long ago because of the drinking. It was the thing that got me sober. Almost lost my job but managed to get my act together. Five years later, I was clean and sober but things got tough at my old company."

"You were afraid of drinking again and that is why you started Dynamic."

Tom looks surprised and sits back in his chair. "You don't miss much, do you? That was exactly why I did it. The stress there was getting too much. At least with my own venture, the stress is mine and not others. I am impressed you figured that out."

"The patterns are the same, I lived with that my whole childhood. You seem like a really nice guy. I think you made the right move."

"I am glad you approve."

"Sorry, I get too direct at times, I guess."

"No worries, you are young. Seasoning comes with age."

They finish their lunch as Tom says, "We better get back before the boss catches us being late."

Vickie laughs as they walk back to the building and to their offices. Mike, the IT guy, has finished setting up her notebook on her desk.

Vickie, "That was quick."

Mike, "Let me show the e-mail and file structure." Mike educates her on the use as she navigates around a bit.

Tom comes by and shows Vickie more of what they do.

Mike, "Let me know if you need anything, Vickie, and welcome aboard."

Vickie, "Thank you, Mike."

Tom, "Thanks, Mike."

Mike leaves as Tom asks, "He get you straightened out?"

Vickie, "I think so, it will take a little while to comprehend how it is all setup."

Tom shows her the ins and outs of the business and leaves her with files to look at. As quitting time approaches, Tom walks in, "So how was the first day?"

Vickie, "Very nice, thank you."

"Well don't keep yourself here, there is always tomorrow."

Vickie closes a folder. "Sure, I will see you tomorrow."

Tom smiles and as he leaves,. "Have a good evening." Tom goes on to see other employees off as Vickie watches. She thinks to herself that this man really enjoys people. She may have found her job. She gets up and leaves for home.

Weeks pass and Vickie has acclimated nicely to her new job. She seems to be picking up quickly on how to do things. A meeting they have been preparing for finally comes today. Seems a large client has given them a chance to hear out their ideas for a new company image. Tom and his team present various marketing campaign ideas as they get shot down one after another.

The client asks, "Those are not bad campaigns, but we sell everything from toothbrushes to artillery for war. The problem is that certain sections of the populace would prefer not to buy home products from an arms dealer. Even though that is a separate division to the home division altogether. We need to soften the image of our home product side of the company. You have anything that can solve that problem?"

Tom and his team look around at each other as there is silence.

Vickie says, "Sir, have you thought about just owning the problem?"

The client looks confused and says, "Young lady, we are trying to avoid that."

"You can't avoid what you sell, the public is aware of it. What I am saying is not trying to hide or avoid it but advertise the fact you sell ammo. Make people very aware you do and that it is something you are proud about because if you did not, some unscrupulous company would. Soften the arms part of your company. Make it seem you are filling the void with your quality. Say it so much that those who protest about it will have no one to rant to anymore. Everyone will know it and won't care eventually. Fact is, companies are here to make money so people just need to quit being infants about it and pick other battles to fight. Stagnation breeds controversy as it grows when nothing is there to keep it out. As far as product quality, the bottom line is that people can choose two out of three options: fast, cheap, or good. They can pick any two but will lose the third. Bring this out in the open and you will wear the issue out and get attention at the same time."

Tom and the other team members are sitting staring at Vickie with mouths open as they pan over to the client. He sits there staring at Vickie and then starts chuckling, then laughs as Tom and the team begin to laugh.

The client says, "Maybe you're right, we shouldn't shy away from what we are. You guys have a week to get me a marketing campaign on it, all right?"

Tom, "Yes, sir, we are on it."

The client gets up and shakes hands as he leaves. Tom escorts him out but quickly comes back to Vickie. "Bold, different, this is your account to project manage." Vickie smiles as she begins to call team members in to start working on ideas.

The next week, the client returns to hear Vickie's pitch.

Client, "Okay, ma'am, what do you have?"

Vickie stands up and starts a slide presentation. "Your company started out making soap. Then it moved to a variety of household products. You acquired a company twenty years ago that made ammo. This company was producing poorly made, cheap ammo that failed often. They were about to go under when you acquired them. Since then you have produced some of the most recommended ammunition even among gun groups. That needs to be told and in this campaign shown that no matter what you make, it is the best. High quality for everyone. Because while a hairbrush you make may not save a life, a good quality bullet used by a homeowner or police officer might. This is your philosophy, this is your standard on all products. Here is what we suggest in making this statement proudly." Vickie outlines the markets and statistics they have come up and where it should be advertised first.

The client asks many questions, and at the end of the meeting, rubs his chin looking at the last slide. "You know, folks, I am going to present this to the board for approval. I think this would work." He stands up and shakes hands with Tom and other team members. Then he walks over to Vickie. "Young lady, I am impressed and that does not happen often. You have a sense of genuineness about you and I like that."

Vickie, "Thank you, sir."

"You will hear from us soon."

He leaves as Tom walks over to Vickie. "I will be right back to talk to you." Tom returns and asks Vickie to join him in his office. As they sit, Tom says, "Vickie, I am adjusting your salary to full standard for your profession. As project manager for this account, you will also get a small commission out of it."

Vickie, "I appreciate it but are you sure you want to adjust my salary with things so tight? This account is not a guarantee."

Tom, "Even if we don't get the account, I want you to be paid in full. I can't afford to lose someone like you."

"Thank you, Tom, I hope we get the account."

"Most likely we will because that man is a heavy stockholder in that corporation so the board will likely follow his lead. Be proud of yourself, you did good."

"I just wanted to be honest about things."

"You know in this business we spend so much money and time trying to figure out how to scare people into buying things. Driving their emotions to need something that they really do not. Maybe people are hungry for truth and plain speaking about things."

"I think companies would have a lot less PR issues if they did."

Tom smiles and they return to work.

A few days later, Tom calls a meeting of the entire staff. Everyone gathers as this is usually not good news. "I am sorry to say, everyone, but I have some bad news. The bad news is that I have no bad news, we just landed the big account today!" Everyone claps and shakes each other's hands. "The client has signed for a media campaign based on our design for years to come. We will be working on this starting now. This means real revenue far more than all our other accounts put together." Someone yells, "Vickie!" and the room chants, "Vickie, Vickie!" Tom smiles at Vickie as she is slightly embarrassed and smiling.

In the months that followed, the campaign has done remarkably well and the company is starting to get more accounts. Tom mentions to Vickie, "We need more staff already. I need an assistant to direct things. I have you guys to project manage accounts, but I need someone to carry out various tasks."

Vickie looks at the ground and then back at Tom. "I know someone."

"You do, someone who can walk in takeoff running?"

"I am sure of it, if they will come."

"Bring them in."

The next day at lunch, John Taylor from King's Way Marketing is eating lunch when Vickie sits next to him.

John, "Well, there you are. How have you been?"

Vickie, "I am fine, I am working for another marketing firm. How are you?"

"It is the usual crap each day. Have to say though you made an impression on Mr. King that day."

"How is good ole Stan, still smells?"

John laughs. "Yea, the same way. What brings you here?"

"I came to see you. How would like to come work for my company?"

"Seriously, I don't know. I have been there a long time."

"I know it is scary when you are used to things a certain way. Trust me, you will thank me. The job is what you are doing now but for a much better boss."

John looks around. "I don't know. Does he smell?"

Vickie laughs. "Not a scent on him."

John smiles. "You know what, I will talk to him. Tomorrow around lunch time."

"I will set it up, here is the address on his card."

Vickie stands. "It is good to see you, John. Hope to see you tomorrow."

John holds the card. "Thank you, Vickie." He looks at the card and at Vickie as she walks away.

The next day at lunch, John shows up and Vickie sees him and greets him.

Vickie, "Hi, John, thank you for coming."

John, "This is a cozy place."

"Here, let me introduce you to the owner, Tom." She escorts him to Tom's office. "Tom, this is John Taylor from King's Way Marketing."

Tom, "Hi, John, hear nice things about you. Come on in."

They shake hands as Vickie, "Well, I will leave you two alone."

Both men say, "Thank you, Vickie." They both laugh as the interview starts.

Vickie is reading material as Tom points John to her office and he walks in.

Vickie, "How did it go, John?"

"I start in two weeks."

Vickie stands up and shakes John's hand. "That is great, John."

"Thank you, Vickie for not forgetting about me."

"You're welcome." Vickie shows John around quickly but lets him go so he can get back to his old job.

Growth Spurts

IN THE MONTHS that follows the company has seen a major jump in growth. John has been indispensable to Tom and John is loving his new job. The season slows down a bit for them and John talks to Vickie, "Hey, Vickie, I wanted to say thank-you for this job. I love it here."

Vickie, "You sure have fit in here well."

"Would you like to come over and have dinner at my place. Not a date or anything, I make a mean lasagna and would love to treat you to it."

"Sure, John, what time?"

"Seven good?"

"That is fine."

"I will e-mail you my address and directions."

John leaves as Vickie smiles. Later that evening, Vickie arrives at John's house.

"Come in, Vickie, thank you for coming. Everything is almost ready."

Vickie comes in the house and John runs to the kitchen saying, "Make yourself at home."

Vickie stares around at the nice well-kept house and sees toys on the floor and on the mantle pictures of John and another woman. "Who is in the pictures?"

John leans around the corner to look. "Oh, that is my wife. Or I should say she *was*. She passed away."

"I'm sorry to hear about that."

John walks to the edge of the room with a dish towel wiping his hands. "It was seven years ago, she died giving birth to our little angel Becky."

Vickie, "Where is Becky?"

"She is at my mom's. My mom insisted babysitting her while we have our date, her words not mine. I think she was hopeful since I never date."

"Yea, I understand."

"You don't have any pictures of your daughter up here."

John comes around and looks. "Lord help me, Mom took them."

Vickie kind of stares and notices two blank spaces where picture frames could have set. John sits the lasagna on the dining table and says, "Dinner is served."

Vickie walks up and sees a nice array of food. "This looks really good."

"Well thanks, I thought about being a cook for a living but just never got around to it. I love cooking though. Used to cook for my wife all the time. Which was perfect because she hated cooking."

Vickie sits down as John dishes up portions on her plate. "Thank you, John."

"You are welcome." John sits down and they begin to eat.

"Mmmm, that is incredible."

"I told you. That is my best specialty. I love Italian food."

They eat for a while and Vickie asks, "You miss your wife?"

"Yea, more than anything in the world. But I have our daughter, and she is the best thing to happen since my wife died. She fills me with love and joy."

"That is great, John, sounds like you are good daddy."

"I try to be, it is hard being a single parent."

"I imagine. I don't think I could do it."

"You, you could do anything. But you might think you can't but when you have that little person depending on you, you find the ability."

"If only every daughter had a daddy like you."

John stares at Vickie. "Yea, I suppose so." John realizing that Vickie has not had a good family life changes the subject. "I am so thankful for you and finding me this job. I was really surprised to see you again."

"I have to admit something to you. When I worked at your old company, Stan had mentioned to me about replacing you."

John slowly chews as he looks at Vickie. "I had a feeling Stan was getting bored with me. I tried to not give him any excuses to get rid of me. I guess I have you to thank even more because if I would have lost my job, it would have been hard to find another in this game. Not a lot of longevity in the marketing world anyway, but at that place I had been there for a while. The one benefit is I could take care of Becky when needed. I suppose that was one thing that Stan did not like—my other responsibility."

"I noticed something."

"Oh yea, what's that?"

"You don't call him Mr. King now."

John looks around and laughs. "You're right, imagine that."

The evening progresses and the meal is consumed. They adjourn to the living room and chat about various things.

Vickie, "This place is so clean."

John, "I am not much on cleaning but my wife she was. She could not stand for anything to be unclean. I guess I keep it up for her." John looks at the ground and back up. "I'm sorry. I don't mean to bum you out."

"It is no problem, John, you are fine."

"The time has gotten away from us a bit."

"Oh yes, I'm sorry to keep you so long. It was just so nice to talk to someone again."

Vickie and John stand up and at that time the door knocks. John opens the front door and his mom and daughter are there.

John, "Hi, sweetie!" He picks his daughter up and says, "Mom, this is Vickie from work."

Vickie walks over to shake hands with her as mom walks in. John closes the door and says, "This is Becky. Becky, say hi to Vickie."

Becky peers out from hiding on his dad's shoulder, and Vickie sees she has Down syndrome. "Well, hi there, Becky."

Becky, "Hi." Becky hides her face on dad's shoulder and pops up laughing.

Vickie, "She is adorable."

John, "Thank you, she is very special to me."

Vickie looks at his mom. "It is nice meeting you, Mrs. Taylor."

Mom looks at Vickie and looks at John turning to move toward the fireplace and says, "That one is a ten, Johnny."

John, "Mom, please."

Vickie smiles as she watches his mom put the two pictures of Becky back on the mantle. She realizes that she took them for the date in case it was a problem seeing the daughter.

John says in a quiet voice, "I'm sorry."

Vickie replies quietly, "No worries."

Mom turns around from the fireplace. "I hear perfectly well you know. Don't need to apologize for me."

John, "Mom guests?"

Mom, "Boy, you think I am stupid? I see her. You think she can't handle a little adult conversation?"

Vickie, "Mrs. Taylor, I can handle it quite well."

Mom, "Well good, because I don't like to beat around the bush." Mom pinches Vickie's arm. "Kind of muscular for a woman, don't you think?"

Vickie smiles at John as John rolls his eyes around.

Mom, "If I had muscles like that my late husband would have never gone with me."

Vickie, "I'm sorry, ma'am, you no longer have John's dad anymore."

Mom looks at John. "Well, probably his dad, there were others back then."

"Mom!"

"Well, it's true. I needed a real man once in a while and, your dad, well, he just was lost when it came to the bed."

"Mom, please!"

"I'm not ashamed of it. He did not provide well, I had to work. I had to do everything it seems."

John just stares around.

Mom, "He was an okay man, I suppose, until he up and had a heart attack on me. I told him to take care of himself but no he had to eat those stupid chicken fried steaks all the time."

Vickie, "I suppose that would do it."

Mom, "You look a little young for my Johnny but healthy."

Vickie, "Thank you but we just work together."

Mom, "Sure. I know how it is. He is still pining after his wife and that is going to kill any chances with you."

"I don't think so because we are just coworkers."

Mom, "All the same, he could not attract a woman in his pathetic state of mind. Reminds me of his father. I guess that is the only evidence that he really is his father."

John looks embarrassed and upset as his daughter asks, "What's the matter, Daddy?"

Vickie looks at both. "You know, ma'am, I don't think your husband died. I think he dug a hole six feet down and buried himself to get away from you."

The room is quiet as John's mom has a stern upset look on her face staring at Vickie. Vickie stares right back as John hides himself waiting for the explosion. Mom bursts out laughing. "My boy, if you don't pursue this one, I am going to kick your butt. Listen, deary, you come back and see Johnny for more dates."

Vickie, "Thank you, Mrs. Taylor. John, I need to leave now okay. Good-bye little, miss Becky."

Becky shying away and then back looks at Vickie. "Bye-bye."

Vickie leaves as the door closes. John just stands there holding Becky letting out a long gasp and his head on the door.

Mom, "Oh don't worry, I didn't do anything to that girl. You better watch out, that woman is a tough one."

John, "I know, tough like you."

His mom turns to face John. "No son, tougher, much tougher. You stay close to a woman like that and you will be okay."

The night ends with Vickie driving home and laughing about the night's events.

The next day, John comes by Vickie's office to apologize.

John, "Vickie, I am so sorry for my mom's treatment of you."

Vickie, "No need to apologize, she and I are a lot alike. Your daughter is precious."

"Thank you. I volunteer at a therapy place for children with Down syndrome I am a bit more fortunate that my daughter is a more functional with Down syndrome. At the place, parents come in for help in understanding it and parents like us try to help the newer parents. It is very difficult for someone who has never dealt with it."

"Will they ever know what causes it?"

"They know a couple of things that cause it. But they can detect it before birth. What is sad is the norm is to tell parents to abort the kid or institutionalize the kid after they are born. I know the doctors are trying to help the parents by bearing the guilt and avoid a lifetime of struggle. But my wife and I could not do it even with the birth risks and her health. So for me after my wife died upon Becky's birth, there was no way in hell I was giving my child up. It was all I had left of my wife. Reality is that Becky was no issue at all. It has been a joy the whole time."

Vickie, "You have a lot to be proud of."

John says, "Oh by the way, my mom wrote you a letter. I have no idea what is in it but she made me promise to give it you." John hands the letter to Vickie.

Vickie, "Don't worry, I won't let it get to me."

John smiles and leaves. Vickie opens the letter from John's mom and it says: "Vickie, I am sorry for being so rude when we met. My boy lives in such a shell since his wife died. He needs to be more assertive. Fact is that I am proud of him and love him very much. I know you are not interested in him. What I ask if you would watch over him. He lets people walk over him too much. Will you please take care of him for his and my granddaughter's sake? I won't be around forever." Vickie stares at the letter and puts it back in the envelope. She gets up and walks over to the paper shredder to feed the letter in it. She then walks to John's office and says, "John, tell your mom for me, my answer is yes."

"Yes?"

"Yes."

"Okay, I will tell her."

Vickie smiles and walks away.

Tom comes into Vickie's office. "Vickie, I just wanted to say these past months have been incredible. You are doing a great job here."

Vickie, "Thank you, Tom. Looks like we are running out of room in this suite."

"Actually, that is what I came to talk to you about. There is another building not far from here on the other side of the park right next to a bookstore. Would you like to come with me and take a tour of it? They have space that would accommodate our growth well."

"Sure."

They leave to look at the new place. As they are shown around by the building management, Tom and Vickie look around.

Tom, "Vickie, I think I would make that corner my new office."

Vickie, "Nice."

"How about that space next to it as yours?"

"That is a nice size office, you sure?"

"It is no question you earned it and everyone feels that way. Because of you we have grown twice our size in months and will grow more. I want to give you more responsibility in managing people, groom you for better positions later. Your advice is invaluable, and I depend on you. You deserve this office."

"I'm honored, okay. I will take it."

"Good!"

As they are leaving, Vickie says, "You already picked out that space, didn't you? That is why John is not with us or your other guys."

"I actually showed them last week and talked to them. Wanted to make sure they were okay with your new office and they were. I actually will be signing the lease this week on it and they will start the build out. In a few months, we should be moved in here."

"Well, it is enough space. You must be optimistic."

"For the first time in years."

As time passes, Dynamic moves to their new office. Vickie is given more oversight of accounts and input into campaigns. The company grows as Tom brings in more marketing people and a new vice president, Dan Childers, to help guide them into growing into the next phase of company. Dan comes from a diverse background and his experience as well as relationships brings things to a new level. Vickie works closely with Dan learning the ropes of corporate culture. As the year progresses, she has managed to finish her master's early. She continues to teach and be instructed by Sato at the martial arts school. Things begin to move smoothly, and Vickie is pleased with her life. She decides to visit late at night an old friend. She climbs on the roof of her old college and finds Professor Jack Chan looking through his telescope as usual.

Jack, "Well, if it isn't the Valkyrie herself."

Vickie, "Hello, Mr. Chan, thing's looking up."

"Yes, looking up. You know how many worlds out there may have intelligent life like ours?"

"Many?"

"More than can be imagined, mathematically speaking."

"Will we have to fight them?"

"I don't think so. The ones we would have to fight would be too far away to reach us. Say, do you think that mathematicians believe when they die there is an aftermath?"

"Ha-ha you are so funny."

"How are you doing lately?"

"I am doing great actually. I think I finally found my place in life."

"Helping people."

"No, marketing and making companies more profitable. Influencing people to buy products. It is quite amazing actually."

"It is good training."

"Training for what?"

"You really think we were meant to just sell things to each other. I think you are meant for much greater things. All this is just teaching you what you need to get there."

"I don't see how, I am happy where I am at."

"You think I went to school to be an astronomer to stare at stars all night?"

"That is all I see you do."

"You are not seeing what I see. I am not looking at stars all the time. I am looking at space."

"Why, nothing there."

"Oh, but you are wrong. Everything is there. Forces we can't even measure are there. I believe that someday we will discover we are in a vast ocean, and space will not even be the correct term anymore. Because it really isn't space or empty but full of things. Just like right now you are focused on the stars at your work. You are focused on what everyone else is. But you know there is something beyond all that that is guiding you and teaching you. You are being prepared and when you see it, the universe will be full."

"You are quite a philosopher. I think that is why I like you. Not a typical boring professor."

"Well, I get romantic about things. Not a lot of people in my field share my views. You would be surprised though to know what many of my colleagues think about in private. There are many that have incredible theories and thoughts about science but one must paddle down the same stream of conventional thinking. Otherwise we are considered crazy and end up teaching at a college somewhere."

Vickie laughs. "You are not crazy, a little off maybe but not crazy."

"Well thank you for that vote of confidence. What would you like to look at tonight?"

Vickie looks at various objects through the telescope.

"Thank you for all your insights and letting me look through the scope."

"You are always welcome. Keep looking up."

"I will." Vickie leaves and heads home.

Valkyrie

VICKIE HAS TAKEN some time off and goes to find Chip. She has lost contact with him as phone no longer works. She arrives at his home and a neighbor tells her that Chip passed away. Vickie is disturbed and upset asking, "How? When?"

Neighbor, "They found him dead of a heart attack a month ago. He was such a nice man. Are you family?"

Vickie, "No, yes in a way. He helped me when was a teenager."

"Yes, he did many. He always had dreams of being a big motivational speaker, but I am glad he never did because there were people he would missed helping. People like you."

Vickie smiles. "Yes for sure."

"He is buried at Chimes Cemetery on Tarking Street. Do you know where that is?"

"Yes, I know where that is, thank you."

The neighbor gives Vickie a hug and Vickie leaves for the cemetery. Vickie pulls in the cemetery and sees the new graves and one marked "Chip." She gets out and looks at a little cross with his name on it. Obviously, he was buried with no stone to mark his place as he never had anything. Vickie cries and says, "Thank you for being there when I needed you. I will never forget you." Vickie kneels before his grave and silently reminisces about him. Vickie then walks over about thirteen graves down and there are the graves of her mom and dad. Vickie says, "Mom, I miss you so much. You were my protector and bore so much so that I would be okay. I forgive you for what you did with my child. I will never see my little girl but maybe it is for the best. My life seems to be just plagued with issues, but I will make myself strong to withstand it. Mom, I will protect myself and others if I can just like you did for me. Dad, I forgive you for the years of drinking. I know you had it hard in life. You tried to make things work but just could never figure out the formula for happiness. I will learn from your mistakes and will be compassionately strong in dealing with anyone like you. I won't tolerate destructive behavior. I will find what my real destiny is in this world. I swear to you, I will." Vickie walks away and back to her car as she passes by Chip's grave. "That is not fitting you." Vickie drives to the funeral home and buys Chip a beautiful new gravestone. The director asks what she would like inscribed on it. Vickie replies: "Motivational Speaker, Mentor, and Loving Father." The director tells her it will be on there in a few weeks.

Vickie returns to work as Dan comes in her office. "Hey, Vickie, do you like these betting fantasy games?"

Vickie, "Like football, so forth?"

"Sort of."

"Not really."

"Well, there is a game that a lot of us execs like to play that I think you would be great at."

"Really, what it is?"

"It is the ultimate in betting games. It is called the Lazarus Game. You know, Lazarus who was brought back from the dead. The game is we all bet in a pool and then we pick for another person, a very poor person and help them become successful at something. There are a lot of rules but basically whoever can get this person to be successful achieving various milestones first, wins."

"What happens to the person after the game."

"Well, they move on with their life, hopefully they remain successful. Kind of helps people and lets them see a part of life they never would."

"Sounds like giving a hungry person just enough food to torture them."

"No, no, no. Not at all. It is all in fun."

"I don't think I am interested."

"Okay, well, suit yourself. I think you would have been excellent at it. We could have allied in the game." Dan lays a paper of the Lazarus game rules on her desk.

"Sorry, my games are for real."

"Okay, well your loss." Dan leaves as Vickie stands at the office window behind her desk. She begins to tell herself, "Leave it alone, Vickie, I have work to do." Vickie looks at the game paper and it has a symbol at the top that looks like a Valkyrie. Vickie picks the paper up and looks at Dan in the distance as she thinks, *Puppet strings work both ways sometimes.*

Other books and information can be found at:
www.Mazzaroth.net

If you have any comments about this novel please
write to: msims@mazzaroth.net
I would love to hear your thoughts. Thank you
for reading my story.

Mike

www.ingramcontent.com/pod-product-compliance
Lightning Source LLC
Chambersburg PA
CBHW031234120726
47905CB00002B/591